FIRST PASSAGE

THE PATH-FORGERS CHRONICLES

This is a work of fiction. Similarities to real people, places, or events, are entirely coincidental.

Contents

Prologue

October 21st, 2244

Nathan leaned against the cold, fogged glass of his bedroom window and looked out at the dark streets below. Mildew ate at the wall under the window. The light that hung from the ceiling gave off an ill yellow glow. A figure entered the street, illuminated by a single dull lamppost. His stomach clenched as he recognized his father. His father clutched a solid black bag that bulged from the contents. Nathan stepped away from the window. He hoped in time to not be seen.

Sitting in the far corner of his room, Nathan rested his head on his knees while adrenaline sent his blood racing. The doors of every closet and cabinet in the apartment were ripped off. His bed lay on the floor, which made it difficult for him to crawl under it. He reached his hand to touch the welt on his back left from yesterday's punishment and flinched from its sting. Black and blue marks in various stages of healing mottled his small frame.

The front door screeched open and banged shut. Several thumps in the kitchen followed, accompanied by a stream of foul language.

Nathan closed his eyes wishing his father would pass out from the liquor already. He just wanted one night without new bruises to cover up in the morning.

"Nathaniel, come here," his father yelled from the kitchen. As ever, luck evaded Nathan's grasp.

He stood up; shoulders tensed. Disobedience would only make his situation worse. He crept into the kitchen and tried to brace himself. The stench of rancid alcohol was almost unbearable. His father paced between the counter and the island table, which was cluttered with empty glass bottles and cans. He spouted slurred, incoherent words while waving his hands in sharp, violent motions that might easily turn onto Nathan.

Dropping his gaze to study the mud-scuffed floor, he tried not give his father any excuse to harm him. Making eye contact or even a facial expression deemed disrespectful was all it would take. From his peripheral vision, he knew his father pointed at him, blamed him. For what crime, Nathan didn't bother to listen. The reason alternated between the sorry state of the house, his mother's absence, his father's over-drinking, something being an inch out of place, or Nathan's existence in general.

The shouting stopped, and Nathan looked up, his blood rushing cold at the sudden change. "I've had enough of this." His father leaned his hands against the counter as a madman's grin curled his lips, and a few deranged chuckles escaped his mouth. Nathan took a step back, more frightened by this behavior than any other outburst witnessed in the past. "I don't want to see those villains ever again. Your mother would still be here. They harass me because of you." His father fixed Nathan with a glazed stare. "If it weren't for you, I'd have control of my life."

His father reached his hand across the counter through the thick mess, clasping on to something. Several glass bottles shattered to the floor as Nathan's father lunged at him. He spun to run, but his father grabbed him by the shirt collar and dragged him to the hardwood. Nathan thrashed at his father's stronger grip. He twisted onto his back panting as he tried to wriggle free. A gleam of silver overhead froze Nathan in a moment of horror. His father held a knife. *He's really going to kill me this time.*

Pain exploded through Nathan, and he screamed in terror. A tingling sensation came to life in Nathan's nerves, and a static burst of electricity shot out from him. His father flailed as he got flung back from the shock wave. The kitchen light burned out with a thin trail of smoke.

Nathan wasted no time to scramble his way into the bathroom—the only room left with a door. He pulled the door closed and locked it. Nathan's breath came in short gasps, and tears filled his eyes. Blood oozed down his torso from a stab wound just under his left collarbone. He sank to the grime-smeared tile and leaned his back against the wall. He grabbed an old, faded hand towel that hung from a bar above him and pressed it against the wound. Blood continued to spill out from the injury.

Nathan jumped as the door shook with the pounding of fists. "Open the door," his father screamed. "Open it, or I'll break it down." Nathan curled into a ball on the floor pressing the towel tighter into his wound. He sobbed while his father continued to bang on the door.

A wave of relief swept over Nathan when the banging stopped. He waited until only silence filled the apartment before he dared to get up. He turned the lock of the bathroom door. A thrill of anxiety rushed in his veins, and he held onto the doorknob. When nothing happened, he pushed the door open and stepped out. His father lay on the couch, passed out with a bottle of liquor still clutched in one hand.

Nathan went to his room, where he tried to lift his backpack and discovered it was too heavy. He emptied the contents and stuffed a couple of change of clothes in it instead. The clothes were barely light enough for his weakened eleven-year-old body to carry. He fought his way into a thin jacket, the only one he had, and slunk through the apartment, past his father to the porch door. He inched the door open. He winced when it creaked and glanced back at his father. Still asleep.

Cold, late-fall air met him as he stepped outside. Dizziness buzzed in his head as he stumbled through the dark streets, hand towel still held against his chest. He planned to get as far away as possible from the apartment and his father.

Three large figures appeared in the street ahead. Nathan stopped, and his heart sank. Wolves. The thick-furred animals took slow, careful steps in his direction. The lead wolf reached him and sniffed at his hand. Nathan closed his eyes, hoping the wolves would leave or finish him quickly.

"Nathan? Is that you?" a small voice cried out. Paws pattered on the ground as the wolves ran away.

A stronger wave of dizziness crumpled Nathan to the ground. The blood-soaked towel slipped from his grip. When his head cleared a little, he tried to pinpoint where the voice came from, but exhaustion held him in place.

"Nathan." He recognized the voice to be of his friend, Summer. Her boots appeared in Nathan's line of vision. She sat down next to him and pulled Nathan into her tiny lap. "It'll be okay. You'll be okay," she tried to reassure him as she pressed the towel to his wound.

Weak sobs racked Nathan as his strength ebbed.

January 10th, 2245

Rain drizzled from the pale gray sky overhead. Josh Black navigated around large, ice-rimmed mud puddles that were scattered in the old rundown alley. His partner Carson Lilton walked almost shoulder to shoulder with him.

"Glad we got assigned the easy job today," Josh said.

"Same," Carson agreed.

He stopped at the end of the alley in front of an old, mildewed, redbrick apartment. Josh took tentative steps up the slippery staircase and knocked on the door. Several minutes passed in impatient tension. Carson pounded on the door harder this time.

Moments later, the door opened to reveal a grungy man who swayed to keep his balance. His eyes carried a glint of anger, and his jaw was set tight with tension. The man's once white T-shirt was stained and moth-chewed. Josh's lip curled from the nauseous reek of alcohol that billowed off the man's breath. Typical behavior for Horace Clouse.

"Whada you want?" Horace asked, looking Josh and Carson up and down.

"You know why we're here. Where is he?" Carson asked.

"Oh, that." Horace's voice was laced with disgust. He began to wring his hands together. "If you're here for the experiment, I'm afraid he's gone."

"Gone? What do you mean gone?" Carson's voice rose.

"I don't know. He just took off one day, haven't seen him since," Horace said.

"And you never contacted us?" Josh drew up next to Carson. Josh crossed his arms, creasing the gray suit he wore.

"I thought he'd come back." Horace shook his head and nearly stumbled over.

"We're going to have to search the apartment," Carson said. Josh and Carson shoved past Horace into the building. Josh's stomach turned at the sight of the state of the interior. The floors were littered with filthy laundry and empty liquor bottles, but no one else was inside.

Josh backtracked through the apartment and noticed several brown smears and drops among the floor litter. He followed the trail to the bathroom, where the smudges looked the worst. "Carson, come here," Josh called.

"What is it?" Carson walked over to Josh.

"Look. The kid might be dead." Josh pointed at the smears.

"Let's not jump to conclusions just yet," Carson said.

"We need to let Reed know," Josh said as they exited back onto the streets.

With a nod, Carson un-pocketed his telecom and placed the call. He got an answer after a few rings. "Hello, Reed. Nathaniel Rune Clouse is missing. There's reason to believe he might be dead. Of course, an investigative team will be sent out immediately."

Chapter 1

December 27th, 2250

A cold winter breeze swept by Nathan and Summer. They walked, each with an arm wrapped around the other's torso, next to an ice-edged river, the middle channel glimmering under the morning sun. A bridge arched over the river ahead of them. A single car rumbled over it. Trees lined the center of the wide pathway they walked, and tall brick buildings rose toward the sky.

Something stirred in Nathan's chest as he gazed over the water. He enjoyed the sight, his companion even better.

Nathan stopped and broke away from Summer, giving her hand a gentle squeeze. He stooped down to pry free a small, iced-over stone on the ground. Tiny cold grains of earth crumbled from the stone against his fingers. He sent the stone skipping across the water. Summer smiled at him. He loved her smile—if only she'd show it more often.

"One, two, three, four, aaand five. Good throw," she said.

"Thanks." Nathan flashed her a grin. He walked back to her and placed his hand on her thin waist. Her black leather jacket, the more elegant twin of his own, was cold to the touch. She reached up to awkwardly lay an arm over his shoulder, pressing closer to him. As long as he continued to have such wonderful moments with Summer, nothing would matter but those moments.

Ahead of them, four trees hovered over an old wooden bench that overlooked the river. Nathan guided Summer to sit with him. Summer's loose blond curls reflected light just as brightly as the river lapping at the bank's edge with quiet burbles.

Summer tightened her fingers around Nathan's hand. "I can't believe how far we've come."

Nathan's gaze rose to meet hers. *How long has it been? Five? Six years?* How time flew. "I wouldn't be here without you," he said.

Summer's gaze shot away from him. "We should go back to base." She stood up and tugged Nathan's arm.

Disappointment echoed in Nathan's chest. *Not yet. Alone time can be so hard to get.* "Let's stay just a little longer," he said.

Summer gave an exaggerated sigh. "Really? We both have other responsibilities, you know?"

Summer meant to the other people who shared the warehouse they lived in. The group who took him and Summer in six years ago after he ran away from his father. People called them Preduals—a batch of loosely associated misfits who'd fallen out of the Union's system, whether by choice or due to circumstances. People like himself who didn't have anywhere else to go to.

"Alright, let's go back," Nathan said.

Reluctance slowed his every step. Summer, several paces ahead, encouraged him to hurry up.

She won't change her mind; he decided and followed a little faster.

Once back at the old warehouse, Summer took off to chat with a couple of Predual girls she'd become friends with. Disheartened by their alone time being cut short, Nathan looked away and went inside the warehouse. An instant blast of thick, musty air assaulted his nose and throat. Despite how much time he'd spent here, he could never adjust to the overpowering smell. He navigated his way through the halls into the lower levels of the building. The handle of a single door differed from the rest. The lock was newer and of more sturdy metal. Nathan entered the room, this being the one he'd claimed as his own, and closed the door behind him.

He went over to an old, scratched-up desk with a scrunched shirt shoved under one leg to keep the thing level. Nathan pulled at the bottom drawer. It came partially open and then got stuck. After readjusting the angle, the drawer opened the rest of the way. A pile of books filled the inside, many he'd gotten from his teacher, Grant. At the very back corner of the drawer, a small gold chest sat, half-hidden by the books he'd placed over it—a Spatial-box, one Nathan created after some experimentation with the sciences Grant taught him. Nathan pulled the chest from the drawer and tweaked a few settings. The chest grew in size. He reached for the lock and released a tiny green spark of magic from his fingertips. The lock clicked open, and Nathan removed some papers from within—incomplete blueprints of the project he kept himself preoccupied with between scavenging jobs.

Nathan glanced over the previous sketches and equations. Someday, he'd present this tech to the world. It would be his way out of a scavenger's sketchy, unstable life. He hoped anyway, as a part of him worried that the Union would reject him as an inventor since his apprenticeship was unarranged and undocumented. Still, that wouldn't deter him from trying to make a life for himself.

Perhaps it's for the best that my time with Summer got interrupted. I have some extra time to work on this now.

Hours slid by as Nathan continued to work on the blueprints of his project. An orb of light, which slowly changed from cyan to green to white, floated above him. Fatigue made his eyelids heavy. He needed sleep, otherwise a mistake could occur on the blueprints. That could be fatal. Another thought jolted him. He also needed to be ready for a scavenging job planned for tomorrow. He'd almost forgotten about it.

Nathan stood up from the desk and stretched. *Suppose I should sleep here tonight,* he thought. *Summer doesn't like it if I wake her.* He cast a glance at a pile of old pillows and blankets in one corner. The makeshift bed would serve its purpose as it had many times.

Before Nathan could lie down, a strange but familiar tingling, like a mild electric current, froze him in place. His immediate reality became dim as his mind got pulled elsewhere. No longer inside the old warehouse, Nathan glanced around. *Where am I?* Tall buildings rose up on either side of him; rain fell from the night sky. Ribbons of blackened water streamed across the ground. His gaze followed the trails of black water to where two large eagles were tearing at a small, half-devoured body.

Horror shackled Nathan in place. One of the birds' heads turned to him. A sharp beak parted in a screech, and its wings lifted over its shoulders. The other eagle looked up as well. The closest predator launched itself through the air at him. Nathan lifted an arm in front of him and took a couple of steps backward as the bird's wings spattered blood onto him. The scene before him blurred together.

The vision ended and lurched him into his room, the real world, where he tripped over his own backpedaling feet. Pain jolted up his spine from the fall, and Nathan took several gasps of breath to calm himself. His whole-body trembling from the experience. Being alone tonight would no longer be okay for him.

Nathan climbed up off the floor and exited the room into the hallways of the old warehouse. Darkness shaded every corner as he navigated his way to Summer's quarters. He finally reached her door. His hands shook as he turned the knob and pushed the door open. He flinched at the sound of the creak the hinges made. A muffled shuffle came from inside the room, followed by a small spark of purple light.

"Nathan?" Summer's voice whispered.

"Yeah," he answered. *Please don't be mad at me for waking you,* Nathan thought.

The purple light grew brighter and revealed Summer's lean form under the sheets she was curled in, lying on a mattress set on the floor. "More nightmares?"

"Something like that." Not nightmares, visions.

Summer shifted; holding herself up on an elbow, she outstretched a hand. Her fingers curled forward and backward, beckoning him. Relief pulsed through Nathan. She hadn't turned him away. He crossed the room and crawled onto the mattress behind her. Wrapping an arm around her, he breathed in the comforting, familiar earthy scent of her long, blond curls. Summer wriggled to press herself closer to him.

"We're safe here. The past is over. There's no need to let it seep into our present." Her voice came quiet with sleepiness. "Ah, don't freak yourself out so much."

"You're right," Nathan said. "Still, hopefully, one day, we'll live somewhere less damp and moldy."

"Mm, I hope so, too." She intertwined her fingers in his.

He closed his eyes and allowed himself to enjoy the butterflies the gesture provoked. "I need to talk to you about what just happened," he said.

"Aren't you leaving to scavenge in the morning?"

"Yeah, but this is important," Nathan said.

"Everyone has nightmares. Go to sleep, and let me sleep, too."

"The vision I just had is bothering me. There was blood—"

"It wasn't a vision. Just a nightmare. Nothing will happen. Now go to sleep." Summer's tone grew harsh.

"But—"

"Don't forget about your mother. You don't want to end up like her, do you? I don't want to lose you," Summer said.

A single uncomfortable jolt pounded within Nathan. His memory drew him back to the deterioration of his mother's sanity. He'd never learned the cause of her decline, but it hurt him that Summer would make such a comparison.

She used to believe in me...

"Good night, Summer." His eyes closed, but his mind still churned. Sleep would be a difficult thing to grasp hold of.

When he got up to get ready to go, Summer sat on the other side of the room, scrolling through her telecom. He wondered how long she'd already been up. He remembered waking briefly from her movement.

"Morning," Nathan said.

Summer glanced up from her telecom but gave an eye-roll and said nothing.

Is she mad about last night?

Nathan got himself ready for his trip in silence. Once he had everything he needed together, he paused at the door. He looked back to Summer. She hadn't paid him any attention in return.

"I'll see you in a few days," he said.

"Okay." She still didn't look over at him.

An ache grew in his chest. She was back to distancing herself from him. He wondered if she would tell him why when he came back. Maybe the time apart would give her some space to open up.

He opened the door and left to go meet with his ride to the scavenging sight.

January 1st, 2251

Wind cut through the falling sleet as Nathan approached a large structure that used to be a parking garage. The place appeared abandoned except for a few dim fires that glowed within. He stepped under the roof out of the sleet and slogged some of the moisture off his jacket. Nearly soaked through, he shivered as he glanced from fire to fire and wondered where his client, Ray, had set up for the night.

He walked toward the closest fire. He weaved through a few small crowds of people who milled about on the first floor as he searched for Ray. They were likely traders, bootleggers, or scavengers like himself. Some people wore hoods, masks, or other means to conceal their identities. Those people were often actively searched for by the Union or involved in higher-end illegal activities. Some of these people worked as hitmen or sold outlawed weapons or drugs. Others were simply known by the Union to be performing undocumented work. They were often referred to as Faceless.

The firearms trader was one such person who kept his face hidden. Only Union officials were allowed to own firearms. Ordinary people could carry weapons, just not ranged ones. As he passed, Nathan overheard snippets of an argument over prices between the trader and a customer.

Nathan swept his gaze over the room again. None of the people here looked like Ray. *He must be upstairs.*

At the bottom of the stairwell, a heavily tattooed trader selling rare herbs and exotic animals sat behind a purple-clothed table. He did a double take as a large white-furred and feathered animal shifted next to the trader.

"Interested?" The trader gestured at the herbs on his table.

Nathan shook his head and pressed through a group of other scavengers loitering in the stairway.

"Who does that kid think he is, shoving past us like that?" One of the scavengers took a step as if to follow him.

Another scavenger grabbed the offended one's shoulder. "Shh, I've seen him spend a lot of time around one of the Faceless ones."

Once he reached the top of the stairs, he caught sight of Ray's tall, lanky figure silhouetted next to a fire in the center of the garage. He stopped next to the fire to let the heat warm him while Ray was still in mid-conversation with a shorter, chubby man. Soon, the two concluded whatever business they had, and the smaller man walked away.

"Busy tonight?" Nathan asked.

Ray turned around to face Nathan. "You're back already?"

Nathan nodded.

"Don't keep me waiting. What do you 'ave for me?"

Nathan set his bag on the ground and unzipped it. He emptied out a pile of various types of scrap metal onto the ground. Ray knelt down to examine the pieces.

"Most of these are decent quality. Thanks for getting these," Ray said. He dug into an inside pocket of his jacket and took out a small pouch that he handed to Nathan. "As promised, 'ere's what I owe you."

Nathan took the pouch. The weight of the contents felt correct. He nodded approval and stowed the pouch away into his own pocket. "Thanks, call me anytime you need something."

He picked up his now much lighter bag and walked over to the large gaping window of the garage. The ice-coated city glowed in patches while the rest lay in silent darkness. He hoped someday Summer and he would be able to live in one of the maintained parts of the city. Anywhere less moldy than the Predual headquarters would be an improvement. Maybe they would if some of his inventions got recognized one day and he could sell them. His gaze drifted to the brightest section of the city, where the Union's main headquarters lay. An unexpected sourness hit his tongue, and he looked away as the imagery of his vision from the night before resurfaced in his mind.

What's that about? He shook his head. *No, maybe I should talk to Grant about it.*

He left the old parking garage and went to a small single-room shop across the street. The shop's shelves contained various old books, ancient CDs, data drives, telecom chips, and a few other random items.

Grant stood near the back of the shop, trying unsuccessfully to help a customer. Grant would be the Faceless that the scavenger he'd passed by earlier mentioned seeing Nathan spend time around. Although Grant chose to be one for very different reasons than most people in the black market. The visage beneath the cloth Grant used to cover his face with wasn't human. Rather, it was canine, much like the ancient images of the Egyptian dog or jackal, as some might call it.

Nathan walked toward the back of the shop. He stopped close enough to eavesdrop on whatever the middle-aged woman was arguing over but far enough away to pretend he was examining a shelf of books.

"I said I wanted a romance book, not a science book. This is like the exact opposite of what I asked for," the woman said.

"You didn't say romance. You said a book about two people making love," Grant said.

Nathan fought to stifle a chuckle and began to actually look over the shelf in front of him. He found a book with a promising title, opened it to the blurb to check, and brought the romance novel to the woman.

"Sounds like this is what you're looking for," he said.

"Oh." She took the book to check it over. "Yes, thank you." The woman turned a scorching gaze back at Grant. "At least someone knows what they're doing around here." She slammed the money for her book on the table between Grant and herself and stormed out of the shop.

Grant placed his hands on the table and huffed out a sigh. "Thanks, Nathan. I don't get why she was so angry."

"Short-tempered? Though, to be fair, I think most people would have known she wanted a romance book, even if she did put it a bit strangely."

"Tch, maybe you should try learning another language."

"I don't need to. Besides, where're you from again?"

Grant straightened up. "Enough of that. It's been a while since I've seen you. I was starting to worry."

"Worry? Why?"

"Because there's much unrest in this city, and you're not exactly invincible."

"Well, I've been fine, just busy. Anything new here?"

"That you'd be interested in? Yes, actually." Grant reached under the table and pulled out a book on advanced quantum psychics. "I know you're already familiar with the subject, but it never hurts to brush up. Especially considering the project you've been working on. How's that going?"

"Good. I think I'll be ready to finish it soon. I just need a few more parts and to run some tests."

"I'm glad to hear, though I do hope you'll be careful."

"I'll be fine."

"And how's the girl you're so fond of?"

"Summer... I'm not sure. She's been...distant lately." The ache returned to Nathan's chest thinking about her.

"I see. That's a shame."

"There is something I wanted to ask you about, though. I had a vision the other night that—"

The door to the shop opened, and someone walked in.

"Actually, it can wait till later when we can talk in private. Maybe in the next day or two?"

"I'll meet with you in a couple days then." Grant pushed the book toward Nathan. "Don't forget this."

"Thank you." Nathan placed the book into a waterproof compartment of his bag and left Grant's shop with a brief wave of goodbye.

Outside, the sun still hadn't reached dawn, Nathan turned toward one of many lightless sections of the city. The dark streets familiar underfoot. The roads and sidewalks were unmaintained, with several holes and sunken areas throughout the brick and cement. A few old, rusted vehicles sat on the sides of the road, unmaintained. They'd been there a long time.

A shuffling noise in an alleyway to his right brought Nathan to a stop. Moments later, a large black shadow ran out onto the street he was on. Silhouetted in the twilight, two long-furred wolves stood and stared in his direction briefly before running into another street. Nathan released a breath he'd been holding and continued his trek; animals didn't scare him much. He'd come to learn that other people were more unpredictable and dangerous than wildlife.

A few blocks from his destination, human footsteps sounded from behind. A figure stepped out in front of Nathan and blocked his path. A glance over his shoulder proved that he was cornered. Both men were armed. Nathan's stomach clenched. This was much more concerning to him than the couple of wolves. He wondered how long they'd waited here to catch someone to rob.

"Um, is there something I can help you with?" Nathan asked the tall man standing in front of him. He was dressed in a dark gray tactical uniform Nathan didn't recognize; it didn't carry the Union's emblem anywhere.

"Nathaniel Rune Clouse?" the man spoke.

"It's him, alright." The person behind Nathan was stockier and dressed the same.

Not a robbery. Crap, these guys are looking for trouble. "I think there's some mistake," Nathan said.

"No, there isn't," the stocky man spoke.

"Let's make this simple," the tall man said. "You can either come with us quietly or die here."

Yeah, those options suck, Nathan thought. "Who the hell are you?"

"That isn't your concern," said the tall man.

The hell it is. "You aren't cops. So, I'm not going anywhere with you creeps," Nathan said.

"We did warn you." The stocky man drew a long steel sword from behind his back.

A hot flash flared as the tall man ignited fire magic in each hand. Nathan's blood pounded as tension cut the air. He dropped his bag to the ground as his hands reached for the sai he carried on his belt.

The steel sword swung through the air toward him. Nathan turned and lifted his sai to deflect the blow. Intense heat scored against his back, forcing him to drop into a roll across the ground to escape the torrent of flame. Cyan electricity ran down Nathan's arms and burst through the air to knock the fire user away.

Instinct sent Nathan leaping back to his feet before the swordsman could stick him with the steel blade. Several more swings of his sword were blocked by Nathan's sai. If Nathan could just find an opening, he would flee. A ball of yellow fire whisked past his face, inches away from making contact. Nathan's gaze flicked over to the fire user.

Within that moment of distraction, a strong force propelled Nathan backward and slamming him against the alley wall. The stocky swordsman held him with a firm grip on Nathan's shoulder, sword poised under his chin.

"That was easy," the swordsman sneered.

In a liquid motion, Nathan's feet lifted off the ground and kicked forward, catching the swordsman in the stomach. He released Nathan as he fell backward to the ground. Nathan took the opportunity to bolt. Before he could run more than a few feet, hot yellow bars of heat encircled him in a cage of fire and brought him to an immediate stop.

"I'll give you one last chance to change your mind before I fry you," the magic-user said.

The sparks hissing off the bars threatened to set Nathan alight. "I won't go with you," he snapped.

The cage of fire began to shrink in on him. Not only did he intend to burn him alive, but also as slowly as possible. Nathan's stomach twisted in horror. Internalizing his focus, he gathered his strength for one last attempt to escape.

Electricity shot out from Nathan in a powerful shock wave. The cage of fire vanished into smoke. His legs shook and gave out. *No, I used too much energy.*

He pushed himself up. The freezing, muddy ground squelched between his fingers as he struggled not to give in to the sudden weakness that racked his body. The fire user lay unmoving in the street. *Good, he's unconscious.*

A flash of steel caught Nathan's eye, followed by a whishing sound. Pain speared at his waist, and he gasped and curled on the ground. Blood poured from a gash in his side.

The other man's sword struck vertically in the ground next to him. Nathan was lucky his aim had been off. He pulled himself away from the blade. Gasping from the effort it took him to turn around to face the man. In an instant, the stocky man rushed to grab the sword.

Nathan stretched and forced himself to grab the sword's hilt. He pried the sword from the mud holding the blade out in front of him in an effort to stop the man's charge. The man didn't stop. He lunged at Nathan, the sword skewering him through the chest with a sickening wet crunch. The man choked, and blood ran from the corners of his lips. Nathan let go of the sword in shock and scrambled backward across the damp ground.

He stared at the man's limp, bleeding form struggling to process what just happened.

Breathing heavily, Nathan forced himself to stand, exhaustion tugging at his limbs. He gathered up his sai and bag not wanting to stick around here any longer than necessary.

The fire wielder hadn't moved since being struck with electricity. Nathan paused next to him for a moment hoping the man was still alive. Only the stench of burnt flesh hit like a hammer turning his stomach. If the man wasn't dead, he would be soon. Blood and rain mixed together on the ground. Nathan's memory flitted back to the vision. A chill seeped into his bones.

Chapter 2

January 2nd, 2251

The first rays of sunlight were at the cusp of the horizon when Nathan finally reached the Predual base. An old building with a faded exterior, peeling paint, and broken windows, it was really a wonder that it still stood.

"Nathan, you're back," said Shawn, approaching him. He was much bigger than Nathan—taller and thicker in muscle, bigger than most adults, too. A friend of both Summer and Nathan, he lived there with them and the other hideaways. Shawn had joined the Predual's about year after Nathan, he'd been in rough shape when he first arrived, but never disclosed his reasons for coming here. Not that he needed to, after all, Summer was the only person who knew why Nathan joined.

Nathan clutched at the wound in his side, yet Shawn overlooked the detail.

"Is everything quiet here?" Nathan asked through clenched teeth as he neared Shawn.

"You bet it is." Shawn clapped Nathan hard on the back.

Nathan staggered forward with a grimace. Shawn grabbed hold of Nathan's chest to keep him from falling. His eyes widened in shock as his gaze traveled to Nathan's blood-soaked clothes.

"You're hurt," he gasped.

"Shh, no one else needs to know," Nathan said. *No need to alarm people or worse, let untrustworthy Preduals know I'm weak.*

"But how? Should I tell Summer?"

"Don't say anything. I'll tell Summer myself. Please." Nathan brushed past Shawn and headed for the entrance.

"Nathan?" Shawn followed a few steps behind him.

Inside, the Predual base was pitch-dark. The air seemed even thicker than usual. Picking through the familiar halls, Nathan went to a narrow staircase leading downward. Shawn's footsteps sounded behind Nathan as he shuffled down them. Turning right at the bottom, Nathan headed to a door down the hallway. His door.

Shawn grabbed Nathan's shoulder as he reached for the handle. In reflex, Nathan jammed his elbow into Shawn's chest to shake him off.

"Dude, what the hell?" Shawn rubbed his sternum where Nathan had struck him.

Guilt flashed through Nathan, and he released a breath. "I'm sorry, I just...I need a moment to calm down."

"I won't say nothing. Just want to make sure you're okay."

Nathan opened the door of his room and stepped through, while Shawn waited just outside the doorframe. Nathan stripped off his rain-soaked jacket and the shirt under it to inspect the gouge in his flesh. He hissed through his teeth as he touched the inch-and-half-long cut in his side. It needed stitches but luckily wasn't deep enough to require further treatment.

Opening a drawer in his small, rickety desk, Nathan retrieved some thread, a needle, and an antiseptic. He sat on the floor and set his focus on cleaning and stitching the wound.

Shawn took a step into Nathan's room his eyes wide.

"It's not as bad as it looks," Nathan said.

"Who did it?"

"Couple of creeps wandering the alleys. I don't know who they were."
He went ahead and gave Shawn a recount of what had happened. "Do
you know where Summer is?"

Shawn nodded.

"Will you get her for me?"

"Be right back." Shawn vanished into the dark hallway, and his foot-
falls faded into the distance.

Nathan closed his eyes and leaned his back against the wall.

More footsteps sounded in the hall. Nathan straightened back up
to greet Summer. But the figure that appeared in the doorway wasn't
Summer. It was Shawn again.

"She says she's caught up in something and'll come down later."

"Caught up with what?" Nathan asked chest fallen that Summer had
dismissed him once again. *Doesn't she care anymore?*

"She didn't say. Are you guys okay? It seems like she's been avoiding
you lately," Shawn went on.

"She hasn't said we're not but...." Nathan said, surprised by Shawn's
unusual observation. The last time he'd seen Summer, it had felt like
old times, but he worried she was still distancing herself from him. "I'll
just...wait for her to come down."

"I'll be outside," Shawn said before leaving.

Several more minutes of waiting alone went by, only for no one to
show up. *She's not going to come.* Nathan made his way over to the
makeshift bed of old, musty blankets and pillows in the far corner of the
room. He lay down and closed his eyes trying to ignore the persisting
ache in his heart.

The sun hung low in the sky, the first evening shadows beginning to sneak across the ground. After last night's unpleasantness, Nathan spent most of the day recuperating. He wished he'd taken the entire day to rest, but the newest Predual member, Katie, had requested some time to practice her fencing with him. They now stood on the far side of Predual HQ where there was enough room to practice in the deserted alleyway.

Katie's brown hair hung down freely while she held her training sword awkwardly and loose in her hand. Her movements were imprecise without strength behind them.

Nathan signaled for her to stop and walked over to her. "Here, try holding like this, you'll have more swing power." He adjusted her hand position, before stepping out of the way.

She made a forward-swiping motion with the bronze sword in her hand. "It's easier to hold on to," she commented.

"Yeah, it should be."

He wondered what brought Katie to the Preduals. She was maybe a year younger than himself, she ought to have been deep into her apprenticeship by this time. Yet, for whatever reason she'd come here. People didn't just come to the Preduals for no reason, he knew that much.

"Nathan."

His head turned at Summer's voice. She appeared from around the corner of the tall building. Her dirty blond curls were pulled back in a tie as if she was planning on training or intended to do some other job that required it to be out of her way.

"Summer, I...guess you've been busy. I thought I'd have seen you this morning," Nathan straightened up as she approached.

"We should talk." Summer turned a glare of ice at Katie. "You need to leave."

Katie shrank under Summer's gaze. "Right away," she said before hurrying off.

Nathan gaped for a moment before returning his attention back to Summer. "That wasn't necessary. You didn't need to scare her."

"Whatever, she's gone now," Summer said.

"What was so important it kept you until now?"

Summer stood still scrutinizing him in a way he wasn't used to from her, like she was sizing him up for some reason. The tension in her stance made his skin crawl.

"Nathan, things are getting dangerous," she started. "There's been some talk that maybe not everyone is cut out to be in the Preduals."

"That's weird. Most people are here out of necessity. They don't have anywhere else to go. As long as there's no internal fighting, I don't see any reason to chase people away. We never have."

Summer huffed out a breath. "It's not that. Look at this." She held her telecom out; a news article was open on the circular screen. The headline caught Nathan's attention: "Nathaniel Rune Clouse, wanted for double homicide. Report any sightings both of Clouse and his accomplices."

A stone dropped into Nathan's stomach. "Homicide... But they attacked me. I didn't mean for them to be killed."

Summer reached out her hand resting it on Nathan's shoulder giving a light squeeze.

"I know. You would never just kill someone unless your life depended on it." She moved closer to him. "So, please understand. The Preduals and myself, we'll be in danger as long as you're here, and agents are looking for you. You're a threat to all of us."

His heart pounded at her words. "Wait, are you suggesting I leave? I can't do that. You, the Preduals, this is my home."

"Ah, I was afraid of this." Summer's grip on Nathan's shoulder tightened. Her right hand thrust forward, and a sharp jabbing pain erupted just under his ribs.

Nathan staggered backward, gaping at the dagger her hand shoved into his torso. His head reeled as memories pulled him back in time. To the night his father stabbed him. The night Summer promised to stay by his side. *No...not you too.*

"S-Summer?" Nathan couldn't find words for the real questions that weighed his mind.

Summer inched closer pressing the dagger in deeper. In a half daze Nathan backed himself against the wall, as Summer twisted the dagger. Snapping out of his stupor he grabbed her wrist. His knuckles turned white. Summer gritted her teeth as she tried to pull her hand away.

"You mean to kill me?" *This can't be real. Summer wouldn't do this to me.*

Summer's eyes were glossy. "I have to," she murmured as tears slid down her cheeks.

Purple electricity crackled across her skin. It ran down her arm, and Nathan's grip slackened as the magic hit him. She pulled her hand back, dislodging the dagger. Sticky, hot blood welled from the wound. Another bolt of electricity lit the air. Nathan's body froze, and white light flashed across his vision, followed by a high-pitched ringing. Darkness swallowed him.

Buildings and streets blurred together as Nathan opened his eyes, head spinning. His chest tight, painful, every breath a shallow gasp.

"You awake?" asked a familiar voice.

"Ah," Nathan groaned. Slowly, his vision and mind cleared a little. He was leaned back against the wall of an alley building. Shawn knelt over him, tight-lipped concern on his face. "Shawn? What...happened? Where's Summer...?"

"S-she thinks you're dead. She wanted me to dump you somewhere, but I realized you were still breathing. We're not that far from the base right now. You've only been out a few minutes," Shawn said in a hushed tone.

Nathan's throat constricted. "Shit, why...?"

"I don't know, but you should get out of here."

Nathan reached a shaky hand to find his telecom but found his wrist to be bare.

A gasp escaped him when Shawn pulled him up to his feet. His vision faded for a second his body shaking in Shawn's grip. Unable to hold his own weight his knees sagged under him.

"I'll help," Shawn said. He scooped Nathan off the ground to carry him. Nathan gritted his teeth, frustrated at his own fragility.

His mind flitted to the night he'd fled his father's home five years ago. He'd survived then but couldn't help but think tonight might be different. With no means to contact his mentor Grant or receive medical attention his options narrowed down to one thing. To die a quiet death, away from those who wished him harm.

Nathan had lost track of both location and time when Shawn came to a stop in the streets.

"I don't think Summer would look here," Shawn said.

"This is far enough...," Nathan gasped, despite not knowing where they were.

Shawn set him on the ground and gave him a wide-eyed stare. "You're weaker. You're sure you'll be okay?" he asked.

"I'll...pull through...," Nathan lied. He knew it was only a matter of time before he succumbed to blood loss.

Shawn sat on the ground next to Nathan and gave his shoulder a light squeeze.

Nathan's throat tightened at the words he needed to say. "Shawn...you can't stay... Summer will be suspicious...if you take too long..."

"But—" Shawn looked at him in disbelief.

He couldn't hide the truth, not even from Shawn. "It's okay...."

Shawn remained stone-still for several more minutes before he heaved a breath and stood up. "Okay, but you better pull through." Shawn wiped at his face as he turned the corner of the alleyway.

Nathan closed his eyes briefly before turning his gaze up to the sky. Dark snow clouds were roiling in to conceal any visible evening stars. *So, this is it?* His own tears came at last, hot at first, before the icy air froze them. Fighting for breath, he regretted telling Shawn to go. Left alone with his thoughts his memory kept replaying Summer's cruel betrayal. Fits of coughs plagued him, and the copper tang of blood coated his tongue.

The chime of crystal against metal rang through the air, echoing around the high-ceilinged gym. Again, then again. Mark prepared for his opponent's next attack. The azure crystal of his sword Saber gleamed in the dim lighting of the gym.

"That's enough," the fencing instructor called over. "It's four thirty, time to go home."

Mark let out a sigh of annoyance. The instructor never let them go even a minute over. Even though this was only practice, he wished they could have at least finished the duel.

Pressing a small button on the handle of his sword, Saber, it retracted into a nonlethal silver cube. Besides the sword form it could turn into various other tools as well. About three years ago, his Uncle James had given him the unusual piece of tech. The last gift he'd received from his uncle before James's untimely death.

Mark took his mask off and cast a glance at his dueling partner, Gavin Malverm.

"Heh, maybe next time."

Gavin unlatched his own fencing mask. He grinned. His dark brown eyes beamed with mischief.

"What? I was totally winning," Mark protested.

He ran a hand over his red-highlighted, black shaggy hair. Mark was sure he'd have won, after all it was Mark's name at the top of the fencing score board, he'd not lost any matches this year. Still, Gavin kept making each win more of a challenge.

"Guess we'll never know now." Gavin nudged him on the shoulder. "I've got to stop somewhere before I go home. I'll catch up with you later."

"Alright, catch ya later," Mark called as Gavin disappeared around the corner of the door.

Since their apprenticeships started, Gavin no longer attended the same classes as Mark, but they remained connected through fencing.

After a moment, he exited the gym and was met by a chill gust of wind carrying the first snow flurries of the storm.

He turned into the back alleyway, a shorter way back home than the main streets. Still stewing over his unfinished duel, he glanced over his shoulder. Hopefully, he'd be among the first practice groups next time, and not the last.

Mark froze as he reached the middle of the alleyway. Just ahead of him, a human figure lay on the ground, clutching their torso, as weak, ragged coughs got swept up in the wind. His hand went for Saber. A press to the side of the handle transformed the cube into a flashlight. The beam of light shone over the blood-spattered ground to the teenage boy, who trembled in pain. The boy closed his eyes against the bright light. Mark tilted the light to the side.

"Are you okay?" Mark asked. *Why'd I ask that? Of course, he isn't okay.*

The boy's eyes shifted to Mark. "Who...are...you?"

"I'm Mark."

Recognition dawned on Mark as he took in the boy's slight frame and golden blond hair. Nathan Clouse. Mark recalled that they used to attend the same primary school. Until one day, Nathan didn't show up. There'd been rumors that Nathan had died somehow, but no definite answers.

"You're Nathan... What happened to you?"

A spasm tore through Nathan's body, and he curled on the earth. When he looked back up, there was pleading in his eyes. "I don't...have time..."

Mark's gaze darted up and down the deserted streets, then back at Nathan. There were so many questions he wanted to ask. Mark knelt next to Nathan. "Try to hold on a few more minutes. I'm calling some- one to help."

He reached into his pocket for his telecom, pulled the device out, and placed a call.

Lily hovered over heavily scribbled-on notepapers laid on an antique oak table. Her long, auburn hair drooped to brush against the writing. She started as a low-tone series of three beeps emanated from her pocket. She lifted the telecom and checked the name on the screen. Odd, Mark knew better than to call her during lessons. Her stomach clenched, and she tapped answer.

"Hi, Mark. I'm still in my lessons. Is everything okay?" she asked.

"No, no, it's not," Mark's voice answered.

"What's wrong? Are you hurt?" That was the first thought that came to her mind.

"No, but I'm with someone who is. Will you come here? We're on Eighth Avenue, close to the gym."

"Okay, but what happened?"

"I'll explain when you get here," Mark said.

"Fine, I'll be there as soon as I can." He had better have a good explanation when she got there.

Lily stacked her notes together and slipped them into a small periwinkle corduroy shoulder bag. She pulled on a thick blue coat and made her way out of the dining room into the house entry.

"Lily, sneaking off without saying anything? You couldn't possibly have finished yet," a deep, patient voice scolded.

"Dr. Bailey, I just got a call. One of my friends is in trouble," she said. Dr. Bailey was a middle-aged private medical practitioner she was apprenticed to. He also happened to be her godfather.

Bailey's eyes narrowed. "And you think it's something you can help with?"

"Someone's hurt."

"Do you know how bad?"

Lily shook her head. Sudden uncertainty tore through her.

"Then you should get going," Bailey said.

"You won't come with me?" Lily asked.

"Weren't you leaving by yourself anyway?"

With a nod and hard swallow, Lily opened the door and ran out into the night. Yesterday's huge drop in temperature allowed the snow flurries to form a thin layer of white across the ground.

Several minutes later, she reached the street Mark told her he was at. Mark was crouched next to someone lying curled on the path. A stone formed in her stomach at the sight.

"Mark? What happened here? Who is he?" she asked.

"His name's Nathan. I don't know who did this," Mark said.

Lily came forward to kneel next to Mark. She lifted Nathan's arm, pressing two fingers against his wrist to check his pulse. Rapid and weak. His fingers jerked. She had thought he was unconscious, but on second glance, he was at least semi-aware.

"Hey, can you hear me?" Lily asked.

"Yes..." Nathan's answer was barely audible.

"That's good. My name's Lily. I'm here to help you," she said.

She extended her senses, using her magic to find the true extent of his condition—torn diaphragm and a collapsed left lung. A pink light formed in her hand as she moved it over the gash in his torso.

"I know it hurts, but you need to try to take deeper breaths." Lily shook her head as she struggled to heal the wound. It was more than her magic could fix. She fumbled through her shoulder bag for a few moments with one hand, then pulled an empty syringe from it.

"You just carry that with you?" Mark asked.

Lily ignored him and inserted the needle into Nathan's chest. She needed to extract the leaked air from his chest cavity.

Within several minutes, she managed to stabilize him, and set to work on stitching his wound. When she finished, Nathan sat up. His eyes wide and frightened as he looked from Lily to Mark uncertainly. He was shaking.

"Nathan, is there anyone we can call for you?" she asked.

His gaze dropped to the ground. "No."

"There has to be someone," Mark said. "Your parents? A friend?"

Nathan shifted, pulling his arms tighter around himself. "I can't go back. Someone...who I thought I was close to did this to me."

Nathan's entire body trembled, not just from the cold either. His hand traveled to the fresh, rough stitches under his ribs. He wanted to run from there. Find somewhere quiet and safe to rest, but his exhausted mind couldn't think of anywhere. Deep down, Nathan knew that even if he could come up with a place, he was too weak to get anywhere by himself.

Mark and Lily exchanged glances with each other.

"I'll take him back to my place," Mark said.

"Mark, we don't actually know him." Lily's voice was hushed.

"We can't just leave him here. He'll freeze." Mark stood and reached his hand out to Nathan. "Come on, let's get out of here."

After a moment of hesitation, Nathan clasped his hand and allowed Mark to help him up. The ground seemed to sway beneath him, but Mark helped to keep him steady.

"Are you going to be able to make it very far?" Mark asked.

"I'm not sure..." Despite the decreased tightness of Nathan's chest, each breath came with knife-like jabs.

"Deeper breaths," Lily said. "You'll be okay."

Stumbling along with the assistance of Mark and Lily, Nathan's mind kept returning to Summer, to Shawn, the men who attacked him, and his recent vision. He struggled to make sense of everything that happened but couldn't.

Somewhere within Nathan, an all-too-familiar hollowness gaped wider. Dying would have been easier. Now, he would have to find some way to reshape his shattered world.

After what seemed like a very long time, they finally reached the destination—Mark's home, an average suburban house nestled in a part of the city that still had electricity. Nathan followed Mark's guidance along the path up to the house.

When Mark opened the door, a wave of heat wafted over them. The hot air stifled Nathan's breath. He couldn't remember the last time he'd experienced indoor heating.

Mark led Nathan through a short hallway into a living room. "You can stay here for tonight. We'll figure out something else in the morning."

"Thank you." Nathan collapsed onto a couch and was out within minutes.

Chapter 3

U pstairs, Mark lay on his stomach, scrolling through the news feed on his telecom. Morning sunlight spread across the carpeted floor of his bedroom. His odd guest was still asleep downstairs. Last night's snowfall proved so deep that Mark's lessons had been canceled for the day. Just as well, as he still needed to figure out what to do with Nathan.

He continued scrolling through the news feed, anything to delay actually getting up, though most of it was the usual boring stuff. A couple of people went missing, a pharmacy robbery occurred, and there was a fire in one of the blackout zones (sections of the city without electricity). He was about to call it quits and get up when a particular headline jumped out at him. His heart lurched in his chest as he read it. Nathan Clouse was being searched for on the charges of a double homicide. Mark flipped himself over and stood in shock.

After taking a moment to process what he'd read, he took off downstairs. Reaching into his pocket, he found Saber and took it out, transforming it into a crystalline sword. He didn't want to use it, but the uncertainty of Nathan's nature made him cautious. As he entered the living room, Nathan jerked awake.

"You're wanted for murder?" Mark asked.

Nathan's eyes widened in alarm, and he sat up. The motion must have made him dizzy because he sagged and lifted a hand to his brow. Once he recovered, his gaze traveled from Mark's face to the sword, Saber. "Seems so... You're going to kill me? Just make it quick. I'm in enough pain..." Nathan ran two fingers along the side of his neck.

Mark's stomach curled in on itself. "What is wrong with you?"

"My life's been destroyed. Don't you get it? Nothing matters. Whether you kill me now or someone else kills me later, I'm going to die." The force behind the words sent Nathan into a doubled-over fit of coughs.

Mark waited until Nathan's breathing returned to normal, though he noticed fresh, wet blood on Nathan's hands.

"Why'd you do it?" Mark asked. "Who did you kill? It must have been someone important."

"I don't know... It was an accident..." Each word came as a strained gasp.

"What happened?"

Nathan's gaze shot back to Saber's blade.

Mark pressed the side of Saber, and the sword retracted back into a cube. Mark sat on a chair across from Nathan and turned his palms upright. "It's okay, I won't hurt you."

The strain on Nathan's face made it clear he didn't fully believe Mark. A few moments passed in silence before Nathan shook his head and gave in, explaining how he'd been cornered and attacked for his refusal to go with the men. How one man had skewered himself and how the other had died of injuries obtained in the fight.

"I didn't mean for them to die. I was just trying to escape, but...maybe I should have just gone with them." Nathan held his head in one hand, his shoulders slumped forward.

Mark's gaze drifted away from Nathan. His uncle James wouldn't have hesitated to help someone like Nathan if he were still alive.

"If what you're saying is true, it was self-defense." Mark stood up as something else came to mind. "If this happened in a blackout zone, how would anyone even know it was you?"

"My blood was on the scene...," Nathan trailed off. "But I've not been arrested before. They shouldn't have had anything to compare the blood to. No, I...I don't get it."

"Last night, you said someone you knew stabbed you. Why?"

"I lived with a group called Preduals—"

"Preduals? You mean those lowlife thugs?" Mark walked a few steps closer to Nathan.

Nathan flinched. "Not all of us—I mean, them. But I was saying...my girlfriend—erm, ex-girlfriend. Well, yesterday she saw the same article you did. Only she decided having me around was too much of a risk and tried to off me." Nathan lifted his green eyes, dull from defeat, to make eye contact. "I am too much of a risk. You should just end it. That's what you were going to do earlier, right?"

"No. I can't do that." Mark took a step back, his stomach turned again.

"Why not?"

"I...no. Do you even hear yourself?" Mark asked.

Nathan's gaze dropped, and he said nothing.

"Look, maybe there's a way to clear this up."

"You think so?" Nathan asked, his eyes giving away his disbelief.

Mark nodded. "First, though, you should wash up. You're a mess."

Nathan crinkled his bloodied shirt with one hand as if only now realizing it might be a problem.

"Come on." Mark gestured to Nathan to follow him.

Nathan stood up carefully and followed Mark to the bathroom.

"Leave your clothes outside. I'll throw them in the wash. You can borrow some joggers and a sweatshirt in the meantime," Mark said.

"You don't have to." Nathan's fingers curled and released a few times.

"It needs done," Mark said.

Nathan nodded and entered the bathroom.

Why is he so scared? Mark wondered.

After throwing Nathan's clothes into the wash, Mark stepped outside. He exhaled a cloudy breath into the chill air and watched it dissipate. His guts squirmed hoping he was making the right choice. *James would have helped him, right?* His Uncle James had been rather outspoken over societal issues. Particularly the limited rights and often unexplained disappearances of magic wielders. Yet, Mark knew there were details he didn't know. His parents refused to let Mark go through his uncle's stuff despite how close they'd been when his uncle was alive. He didn't even know if Nathan *was* a magic wielder, let alone if that was the reason he'd been targeted. *Maybe I shouldn't have gotten involved.*

Mark pulled his telecom from his pocket. Perhaps it would be best to call Nathan in. He tapped the first number of the emergency code but hesitated. Nathan may have been stabbed by his girlfriend, but the wanted article meant Nathan must have pissed off someone with power. *If I call him in, especially if he is a magic wielder, he might be killed.*

A shadow appeared behind him.

Mark startled and spun on his heel. The person was lean and taller than Mark, taller than most people. Their clothes were casual winter attire, a zippered jacket, and gloves. However, the thing that stood out was the black cloth covering their face.

"So, this is where Nathan's ended up," the person said.

"Who are you?" Mark asked his pulse ticking up as he wondered if they'd been followed last night.

"An acquaintance of his. What will you do now?"

"I...he's dangerous to be around, isn't he? How'd you know he was here?"

Mark flinched when a low growl came from the person. "Doesn't matter. Are you going to finish dialing that?"

He glanced down at the telecom in his hand. "I should. Shouldn't I?"

The man tensed. "Do you think what's happened to him is fair? Do you think he lied to you?"

Mark shifted in place. "No, but—" Mark thought of his uncle again. He wondered what events led up to his uncle's murder and whether someone had given up his location.

Mark darkened the screen of his telecom and slid it back into his pocket. "I'll try to let him rest another day or two, but I can't risk anything beyond that."

The tension left the man's shoulders. "Good. This world may suffer if he dies."

"What do you mean?" Mark asked.

The cloth over the stranger's face pulled tight for a moment as a breeze swept past. Fear froze Mark in place at the sight of an elongated face with the hint of fangs visible through the fabric. Mark took a step backward to gain distance, but the person turned away to walk back toward the inner city. Mark stared after the stranger questioning if he'd only imagined the sight.

Nathan massaged his aching chest as he watched snow glitter and fall outside the window, illuminated by streetlights. Reality seemed distorted to him, too slow and too bright for the turmoil that slithered within his being. The scene made everything feel even more unreal to him—that somehow this was just a nightmare he'd soon wake from.

Nathan's hand found the small, round, red stone in his pocket. He wrapped his fingers around it, and warm energy spread into his palm. Besides the clothes on his back, this stone and his sai were the only items he still possessed. Shawn had left the sai with him, and the red stone must have been overlooked by Summer. Nathan breathed a sigh of relief that Shawn was the one given the task of disposing of him. Anyone else and Nathan would have been left with only magic to defend himself.

A noise on the other side of the room drew Nathan's attention out of his thoughts. Mark stood at the entrance of the doorway. Mark's black-and-red-streaked hair stuck out in places as if he'd been outside.

Mark took a few steps into the room. "Nathan, I, well...my parents will be home soon. I won't call you in, but I don't know how they'll feel about this."

Parents, of course. Memories of nights full of screaming and bruises to hide the next morning flashed through Nathan's mind. "I should leave," Nathan said.

"You'll die if you go now," Mark said.

"I might die if I stay." Outside, the headlights of a car turned onto the silent street. "Is that—?" Nathan backed away from the window.

Mark stepped up to the window to check. "I think so. Wait here."

Nathan wandered to the couch and sat. He studied the carpet's pale cream color. Well aware that his life hung by a strand of web, the hair on his arms rose as he wondered how they would react to him. Mark might have been willing to give him a chance, but that didn't mean his parents would be as understanding. A chill draft rushed through the house as a door clicked open and then closed.

"Mom, Dad." Mark's voice carried through the house.

"Hey, kid, everything okay?" a male voice asked.

"Erm, you see, last night on my way home, I...there was someone injured, and I brought them here," Mark said.

"What? Did you know them?" a female voice asked.

A golden-brown-skinned man with black hair that matched Mark's entered the living room. Mark's father fixed Nathan with a hard stare.

Nathan shuddered as ice crept into his veins. "Hello, sir."

"Who are you?"

"I'm Nathan."

"What happened to you?"

"I got stabbed." Nathan shifted in his seat and wished he could disappear.

Mark came back into the room, followed by a short, plump woman.

"Stabbed? Where? Is it bad?" Mark's mother pressed past her husband to get a look at him.

Nathan cringed as she encroached on his personal space. "It's been treated. Please don't..."

Mark's mother took a step back, and Nathan relaxed a little. Mark's mother swept her gaze over Nathan for a long moment, and for some reason, the beginnings of tears formed in her eyes.

"Who stabbed you?" Mark's father continued to press.

"My ex," Nathan said.

"Why?"

Nathan looked toward Mark, but Mark stared at the floor and offered no help.

"I'd rather not talk about it."

"Why haven't your parents picked you up?" Mark's father asked.

"I don't live with them."

"Then where do you live?"

"I lived with my ex."

"Deviant, huh? You're at least apprenticed to someone, right?"

"Yes." Nathan figured that although not official, Grant would count.

"Can you contact them?"

"I can't. My ex stole my telecom."

"So, what am I supposed to do with you?"

"Nothing. I was leaving anyway." Nathan got up.

The ache in his chest grew worse. He stepped past Mark's parents and headed for the entrance. A hitch in his breath sent Nathan into a hoarse series of coughs, and he stretched his hand to support himself against the wall. The copper tang of his own blood turned Nathan's stomach. He lifted a hand to his mouth and sank to the ground as pain buckled his knees. After a few moments, his breath eased, and Nathan stared at the red spatters of blood he'd hacked into his hand.

"Dad, he'll die out there." Mark moved to stand between his parents and Nathan.

Nathan looked up, shocked. He waited for Mark's father to strike out in anger at the opposition. To his surprise, the retaliation never came.

"Alex, the boy's skin and bones. And he's hurt. Just look at him," Mark's mother said.

"Jeanna, people like him only ever bring trouble," Alex said.

"Just let him stay the night," Jeanna said.

Alex's gaze flicked between Mark and his wife, then back to Nathan. "Fine. You can stay for the night. However, you have to move on tomorrow."

Nathan glanced back at the blood in his hand. *I really could use the extra rest.* "I will. Thank you."

January 4th

Morning sunlight spread into the living room. Nathan stretched on the couch, testing the boundaries of his wound. He cast a glance toward the room's exit. The scent of eggs and meat being cooked seeped through the doorway.

Nathan's stomach cramped in hunger. *Don't expect anything. They agreed to let me stay for the night, nothing more,* Nathan told himself.

Nathan slouched as dizziness reminded him that he'd been restricted to rations during his scavenging trip. And the last couple of days, he'd been too ill to even consider eating.

I need to eat, even if it means leaving. He got up and stepped into the entryway. As Nathan passed by the kitchen toward the exit, Jeanna stepped out of the kitchen behind him.

"Hey, where are you going?" she asked.

Nathan lifted a hand to motion toward the door. "Leaving. Alex said I had to leave today, so—"

"No, come here. You're too skinny to leave now."

"Isn't it better if I go sooner than later?" Nathan reached for the door handle.

"No. You're staying a little longer."

Nathan flinched when Jeanna reached to grab him by the elbow.

"Come on. You're hungry, right?" She gave his arm a gentle tug toward the kitchen.

Nathan's stomach overrode any arguments he might have come up with. He followed Jeanna into the kitchen.

Mark already sat at the pinewood table, his plate over half gone. "You're finally up?" he asked.

"Well, yeah," Nathan said.

"Nathan, what is it you've been doing?" Jeanna asked.

"You haven't been in school. How'd you even get an apprenticeship?" Mark asked.

Nathan hesitated. "I...um...work as a scavenger. My apprenticeship is kind of unofficial."

Jeanna appeared beside Nathan and pushed a plate piled with food into his hands. The plate held more than Nathan would have taken, but he knew he'd eat every last bite.

"Sit down. Eat," she ordered.

"Thank you," Nathan said before sitting at the table.

"That's dangerous work. But what are you training in?" Mark asked.

"Quantum physics," Nathan said. *The data for those projects are still at the Predual base. I have to get it back.*

"You must be clever then," Jeanna said.

"I suppose." Nathan dropped his gaze as heat flushed his skin. He turned his attention to his meal. The rich flavor of the meat proved to be venison, one of the most popular meats due to its accessibility.

"I'm apprenticed as a computer coder," Mark said.

"Hm, is that what you wanted?" Nathan asked.

Mark's mouth opened and closed again. It seemed Nathan's question struck a chord. "It's what I'm good at."

Yet, it's not something Mark actually enjoys. Figures. A resentful memory flashed into Nathan's mind—one of the teachers and faculty pushing him toward the military starting as early as age four.

"I mean, if I could choose, I'd rather be a car designer," Mark said.

"That's a dead-end job, Mark. Besides, people who switch their apprenticeships late normally fail," Jeanna said.

"If you'd stayed in school, what would you have been training for?" Jeanna asked.

"Military," Nathan said. Shocked stares met his answer.

"I didn't think kids training for military were allowed to be enrolled in mainstream schools," Jeanna said.

Nathan looked down at his plate to scrape the contents around. "No one ever said anything one way or the other about it to me."

"It seems strange," Jeanna said. "Was your family military?"

"I don't actually know much about my family."

A subtle but familiar energy current came to life within Nathan. Everything around him began to gain a surreal quality. *Not now.*

Jeanna looked at the slim silver watch on her wrist. "Oh, look at the time. I have a meeting I need to leave for. Mark, make sure you aren't late for your classes."

Mark stood up and sighed. "I won't be."

Jeanna gave Mark a short hug and left.

Reality melted away as Nathan's mind slipped into a new space. Another vision, and so soon after the last. He stood in an unfamiliar place, some kind of underground corridor. Someone stood further ahead down the corridor; he recognized the person's features even from the distance—Mark. Inky black shadows crept along the ceiling and around corners and doorways. Mark walked to one of the doorway entrances. The inky shadows slid toward the doorway.

"No, wait," Nathan called out, but Mark didn't seem to hear him and kept going.

The inky shadows slithered after him, and moments later came a pained cry. Nathan rushed to reach the doorway, but the inky shadows converged on him from all angles; they surrounded him. He cried out in shock as the shadows crawled up him, sapping his strength and obscuring his sight.

The real world rematerialized, and Nathan found himself sitting on the kitchen floor, gasping for breath, while Mark stared wide-eyed at him.

Chapter 4

Nathan stood back up. His hands shaking, as he avoided Mark's eye.

"What the hell was that?" Mark asked.

"I just...nothing. I don't feel so well."

"Don't feel well? You just froze up unresponsive, then fell. You don't think it's because of your injury?"

A shiver ran up Nathan's spine. He'd never had a vision in front of anyone besides Summer until now. *I don't know what to tell him.*

Silence fell. Mark stared, waiting for an answer.

"That wasn't a... Do you have seizures?" Mark asked. "I can call Lily. She'd know what to do."

"No. I'm okay," Nathan said. *There's no way I can explain any of this to him without sounding insane.*

Mark frowned and took his telecom out. He scrolled through the screen for a moment, found a scrap of paper, and wrote a number down. "I gotta go before I'm late, but this is Lily's number. If that happens again, you should call her." Mark went to the entryway and opened the door.

An icy tremor of premonition shook Nathan, and he followed Mark to the door. "Maybe you shouldn't go today...," Nathan faltered when Mark furrowed his brow at him.

"I have to." Mark shook his head and closed the door behind him.

Nathan's blood was racing, spurred on by his vision. He peered out the window along the side of the door. A black van was parked on the street just a few yards off from being in front of Mark's house. Dread twisted his stomach. Somehow, he knew it could only mean trouble. *I need to find a way to help.* Nathan turned and walked deeper into the house and found a back exit. *That'll work.*

Once outside, Nathan navigated through the yards until he crouched in winter-dry shrubs next to the black van. His body shivered as his heat got sucked away into the snow drift between him and the shrubs.

The van door opened, and someone wearing a gray vest walked onto the sidewalk and cut off Mark's path. "You there, you live here?" he asked.

"I don't have time. I'm late." Mark dodged away to skirt around them.

The agent cut off Mark's path.

Flat, round disks perched along the sides of the van—cameras, likely on the front and back of the vehicle, too. Every hair rose as Nathan activated his magic and willed it to fry the van's electrical circuits to the cameras. *No more cameras, no fear of getting caught,* he thought.

"Hey, I'm talking to you. Does Alex Mortain live here?" The agent held up a badge, though Nathan couldn't read what it said from his distance.

"Why?" Nervousness crept into Mark's voice.

"Is he here?" he asked.

"No, what do you want?" Mark asked.

Nathan took the opportunity to slide out of the bushes and crawl underneath the van. Wincing as his sore chest brushed against the ground.

"He isn't here? Who are you? Why isn't he here?"

"No... I just said..." Mark took several steps backward.

"When will Alex be back?" the person asked. "You know him, right?"

"He's my dad. I'm not sure. Sometime this afternoon," Mark said.

"You don't know? He's your dad, right? Are you trying to cover for him? Who are you?"

"N-no, I-I'm Mark."

The person reached behind himself, pulled forth a military-grade energy gun, and aimed it at Mark's chest. "I think I should bring you in for questioning."

"What? I don't understand." Alarm spiked Mark's tone.

Seems like this'll be necessary. Nathan took one of his sai and punctured the gas line. For good measure, he scraped the rubber off some nearby wires.

Nathan glanced back at Mark and the agent. The agent shoved Mark to the ground and cuffed his wrists together.

The agent dragged Mark to the back of the vehicle. The door opened, followed by several bangs as Mark was forced in. Nathan scooted closer to the van's rear.

The back door slammed shut. Nathan turned under the vehicle so he faced the end and grabbed onto some sturdy undercarriage. The driver's side door slammed closed as the agent got back in. The engine turned over, and the van moved forward.

Nathan clung hard to the undercarriage, his heart thudded in his chest. Nathan reached and climbed to the rear end of the vehicle, careful to hold himself up as far from the ground as possible. He soon ran out of distance. He opened one hand, and a small ball of cyan electricity formed in his palm. The spark shot to the front of the van where the gas line leaked.

Fire erupted, and the van skidded. Nathan lost his grip and rolled behind the van across the pavement. He lay still while the world spun. After the dizziness lessened, he pushed himself to his hands and knees.

Several gashes oozed blood. Ragged coughs shook him, and the copper tang of blood hit his tongue. Shaking from the effort, Nathan climbed to his feet. *I can still breathe.* He walked to the van. The front now smashed into a bent pole with fire licking its underbelly. The driver lay slumped over the airbag.

Nathan went to the back of the van, stuck the point of his sai into the lock, and set to work. After a few attempts, something in the gears popped and clattered. Nathan tried the door, but it only came partially open. A good yank ripped the door open the rest of the way.

"Nathan?" Mark's eyes were wide and frightened.

Nathan nodded and took a good look at the inside of the van. The back of the van contained several sets of restraints, chains, and cuffs. A mobile holding cell for multiple people. Mark sat on the floor, his hands pulled behind him, cuffed to a chain attached to the van wall.

Nathan inspected the cuffs around Mark's wrists. The cuffs didn't seem to take a key. Instead, there was a chip-coded electronic device.

Nathan wrapped his hand around the lock. He closed his eyes as he focused on the device and let a small trickle of electricity flow from his hand. *Please work.* The cuffs clicked open as he activated the internal code, and he breathed a sigh of relief. The irritation in his lungs sent him into a brief fit of coughs.

Mark rubbed at his freed hands. "How'd you do that?"

"Worked with enough electronics," Nathan said.

Mark stepped out of the van and stared at the now-dying flames near the front. "You did this?"

"I did."

"They're...a-are they dead?"

Nathan glanced at the front of the van. "Maybe."

"I-I don't understand why they came here. He mentioned my uncle. Why now? Unless this is about you..." Mark's breath quickened, too quick.

"Hey, slow down," Nathan said.

Mark shook his head and lunged forward to grab Nathan by the shoulders. "Who the hell are you?" he screamed.

Nathan flinched. "Get off me."

Mark gripped Nathan harder. "Y-you were acting all weird earlier. Then this guy shows up." He pointed at the van. "T-then yesterday there was this creepy guy with fangs...and something about suffering..."

"What the fuck?"

Mark released Nathan and half-sat, half-fell to the ground. Mark inhaled deeper but still too fast. "Y-you acted like you knew something was going to happen.... Did you?"

Nathan shuffled from one foot to the other. The commotion had drawn a few of Mark's neighbors into their yards.

"I just had a bad feeling." Nathan kept his voice low. "Who was this person with fangs?"

"I don't know..." Mark drooped his head onto his knees.

Nathan suspected the person might be Grant, though he didn't know how Grant would have known to come here or why he would have bothered. A burning sensation in Nathan's chest shook more coughs from him. He spat blood onto the pavement.

Mark looked up, his breath back to normal. "Your injury's worse."

"Yeah, and we've got the attention of most of your neighbors," Nathan said.

Mark grimaced and stood back up.

"That guy, he showed you a badge. What did it say?"

"Union Recruiter/Investigator," Mark said.

"Union...well, shit. All of this is definitely going to cause trouble..." Nathan regretted that he hadn't checked the IDs of the men he'd been attacked by. "We need to get out of sight." A heavy thickness caught his breath, and Nathan heaved another mouthful of sticky, red blood.

"Let's get in the house."

"I don't think so," Nathan said.

"Why not?"

"This place'll be crawling with backup soon. Someone's probably reported this by now."

"What else can we do?" Mark asked.

"I'm leaving. Now."

"But—"

"Mark, if you stay here, you might be killed," Nathan said.

Mark looked away. "No, I won't. I'm going to call my parents."

"I hope you're right. If things look bad, come find me if you need to," Nathan said.

"Where?" Mark asked.

Nathan shook his head. "Wherever I find that seems safe. I doubt I'll get too far. You'll just have to look."

Mark took a telecom from his pocket and tapped the screen a few times. Nathan turned away to walk through the neighborhood. It wouldn't be safe here for him much longer. He cringed at the curious gazes of Mark's neighbors. Soon, he found an alley to slip away into and get himself out of sight.

Mark sat on the bottom step of the staircase in his house's entryway. His parents were on their way home. Mark's stomach twisted in knots as he wondered what would happen next. He watched out the strip of glass along the side of the door for his parents' vehicle.

A black car and an emergency vehicle drove down the road and stopped next to the black van. Mark tensed. His nails dug into the wood of the staircase. Several people exited the vehicles to examine the scene. Mark hoped none of them would come to his house. Another car came down the road and turned into the driveway—his parents.

They got out of the car and walked to the house; his mother reached the door first and opened it. Mark stood and hugged her, relieved to not be alone.

Before his father could enter the house, two of the men examining the crashed vehicle walked over. "Hey, aren't you Alex Mortain?"

Alex stopped on the walkway. "Yes. Any reason you want to know?"

"Know anything about what happened here?" one of the men asked.

"No. I only just got home," Alex said.

"See that crashed car over there?"

Alex nodded.

"One of your neighbors said two people fled the scene. One of them went into your house."

Mark looked down as his mother grabbed his arm tight. She pulled him deeper into the house. "Mark, take what you can and leave quickly," his mother said.

"You're serious? Why?" Mark met her gaze, shocked.

Jenna's lips tightened in a grimace. "Your uncle's death wasn't chance. He was killed by them." She pointed outside. "If they suspect you were involved in that crash, they'll..." Tears formed in the corners of her eyes.

Mark swallowed hard; he understood. He ran upstairs and threw a few items into a bag, hoping it was enough. Mark returned downstairs;

outside, his father was in cuffs, and his mother spoke to one of the agents. Mark's throat tightened, and he looked away.

He went outside through the back door, where he found Nathan's tracks from earlier. Mark followed them a few steps before veering away into a strip of trees behind his house. He knew there was a stream back here that would be frozen, over which he could walk down. Mark reached the stream and tested the strength of the ice with one foot before fully stepping out onto it. He walked along the frozen stream, hoping he would have time to put some distance between himself and the agents before they found his tracks in the yard.

The slams of vehicle doors carried through the air. Mark wanted to go back to find out what had happened to his parents. He took a shaky breath. He couldn't go back. He'd have to find out later.

For now, he needed to find Nathan. Mark wondered how far Nathan may have gotten already. His fist clenched. He didn't know how to survive in the streets.

Josh Black stepped out of the car with tinted windows and inspected the crashed black van. Med techs pulled the agent out of the van to check whether he was still alive or not. Josh entered the van and pulled out the memory card for the van's surveillance. He inserted the card into his telecom to check what had happened, but the cameras had gone out before the accident.

He walked away from the van to his fellow agent, Carson, who was speaking with an elderly woman. Carson turned away from the woman as Josh approached.

"Any footage?" Carson asked.

"No, the cards fried. Nothing on it at all." Josh handed the memory card to Carson so he could double-check it.

"The woman said two boys fled the scene. One went to that house." Carson pointed to the house. "The other went that way out of the neighborhood."

"We don't know that it was Clouse."

"No, we don't, but whoever lives in that house might," said Carson.

As Carson spoke, a vehicle pulled into the house's driveway, and two people stepped out. Carson moved to intercept the man before he could go inside.

Josh hung back for the moment, all this trouble over a boy presumed dead for years. Yet if found, he would certainly be dead. Despite his training, situations like these made doubts creep in.

"Black." Carson's yell snapped Josh back to the present. He went to help Carson restrain the couple for further questioning.

Chapter 5

Nathan eventually found a house that looked out of the way enough to be safe for the night. The houses on either side were also abandoned, the siding mostly stripped away; the house to the left had a gaping hole in the roof. The day's events replayed over and over in his mind. Nathan walked closer. His foot slid under him on a patch of ice, jerking him out of his thoughts. He regained his balance and shook his head at his own carelessness.

After checking for signs that no one else was there, Nathan entered the middle building. Floorboards creaked under his feet as he walked into a dusty living room with only a few pieces of broken furniture. He checked the doors inside the house, hoping to find a basement, but the house didn't have one. The other abandoned homes looked similar, and he doubted they would have one either. Too tired to continue searching for shelter, he decided he'd have to make do here for the night.

He picked up the pieces of broken furniture and shoved them into a fireplace on one side of the room. He winced at the sharp pain in his ribs from his injury and sat down to catch his breath.

He couldn't help but wish that Lily's healing ability had been more effective. Still, it was at least enough it'd kept him alive.

His time spent at Mark's home brought old memories to the surface at full boil. "You'll never amount to anything; if I'm lucky, you'll be gone one day, too." The words Nathan's father screamed at him after his mother got sent to a psych ward echoed in his mind. Unlike his father, Nathan missed his mother. Tears burned his eyes. It still hurt, even after so much struggle to separate himself from the past.

Now, despite his efforts, he doubted any positive future existed for him. Anger burned through Nathan. He hated that his father might turn out to be right.

He longed for a stable and comfortable life, one where he didn't have to constantly watch his back or worry over his next meal. He'd wanted Summer to be a part of it, but his relationship with her would never be the same. He couldn't just live like before, either, not with the Union tailing him. He needed a way to clear his name. Otherwise, he would eventually be caught, and when that happened, he would either be imprisoned, maybe sent to a psych ward like his mother, or executed. He must have pissed someone off, though he didn't know who. Mark was probably right—that it was someone important, or at least someone with connections. He couldn't imagine the Union getting involved over an insignificant scavenger, such as himself if they didn't.

He took the small red orb from his pocket. He'd found it two years while scavenging. Warm energy, laced with a harsher undertone, seeped from the orb into Nathan's hand and spread into the rest of him. Taking a second to focus, he activated his magic. A small flame appeared floating above his hand. The fire slowly alternated colors—green, cyan, and white.

Nathan guided the flame toward the collection of broken wood, but the flame fizzed out before he could light the furniture. He shook from the effort. He didn't have the energy left to use magic. He lay down on the floor with his back to one wall. He needed rest to be able to come up with any solid solutions. Shivers shook him as he fell into a fitful sleep.

"Nathan. Nathan, get up."

Consciousness surfaced at the edges of Nathan's mind. The voice speaking to him sounded distant. His awareness increased, along with a sense of being weighed down by something heavy and cold. *The heavy cold is my body.* The realization sent a thrill of shock through Nathan.

Nathan's eyes opened. Grant's canine face hovered over him. Grant sat beside him, trying to rub heat back into Nathan's limbs. Weakness ached through his body. He began to drift again as exhaustion overwhelmed him.

"Stay here. Stay with me," Grant said. He reached a gloveless, clawed hand into his shirt and pulled out a small, circular, flat piece of metal with a glowing red swirl in the center. He lifted Nathan's shirt up to place the thing on Nathan's chest.

The bit of metal stuck to Nathan's flesh before releasing a thunder-clap-like jolt into him. Nathan's entire body jerked, and moments later, he was curled on his side in the fetal position. Warmth slowly spread back into his limbs, and his exhaustion lessened. Even the air he breathed felt somehow cleaner. A glance at the piece of metal stuck on his chest showed the swirl glowed green instead of the earlier red in its center. Nathan sat up and leaned himself against the wall before bringing his gaze back to Grant.

"I think I'm okay now," Nathan said.

Grant nodded and reached to remove the small device. The bit of metal came free easily with no marks visible. Grant placed the device back under his shirt and took a deep, gasping breath.

He must need that to survive, but he used it on me. "I-I never knew," Nathan stammered.

Grant tilted his head. "It's okay. This device is meant to stabilize homeostasis, an advanced life support. I can go without it for several minutes, but the air here is toxic to me. Going a few moments without it to reverse your hypothermia is nothing."

"I wouldn't have even realized before... Thank you, Grant," Nathan said. "How'd you find me? And why?" Confusion drew the question from him.

"I overheard a rumor you'd been killed, but I have keener senses than some. So, I went to investigate. I have no desire to see you dead. Not to mention how many times you've helped me before. I feel I still owe you a few favors. As I always have, I believe you possess a great amount of potential. It would be a shame to just throw that aside so carelessly."

Nathan's thoughts ran dark. "What's the point? I'm going to be locked in a box or executed."

"So, you're going to give up and let yourself be killed?"

"Summer tried to kill me..."

Grant's lips curled to show his multiple sharp teeth, and his pointed ears swiveled back. "Listen to yourself. What is it you want? Do you want to die?"

Nathan fell silent and looked away. No, he wasn't ready to just give up. He would find a way to get through this. The first thing on his list was to find better shelter. His choice had been reckless. He would find somewhere with an underground basement like he'd wanted to in the first place, and then he'd be safe from freezing. That would give him more time to figure out why someone wanted him dead.

"I'm not sure what I want anymore. I think I'm going to have to find out who ordered the hit on me," Nathan said. "It's just...everything I was working toward, it's all falling apart."

"I'll try to give assistance where I can, but understand I'm not here to get involved with Human politics," Grant said.

Grant reached forward to pick something off the ground. The red orb gleamed in the dim moonlight as he held it in his claws. He turned the orb, inspecting it. Then he extended his hand to Nathan. Nathan reached out, and Grant dropped the orb back into his cupped hand.

"I'm sure that isn't the only one you have by now. Be careful. It doesn't appear to be immediately dangerous, but there's still a subtle sinister energy attached to it." Grant stood up and pulled the black cloth that lay down his back over his head to cover his face. He also readjusted the leather gloves that hid his claws.

"You're leaving?" Nathan asked.

"I'll be around, but there's little else I can do here," Grant said.

"Before you go, I'd wanted to talk to you before. I-I've had some recent visions, and...they seemed sort of cryptic."

Grant sat back down and uncovered his face once more. "I can't interpret them for you, Nathan. You're the seer. But I will listen."

"I know, but it's not easy for me either. Some of the stupid things are metaphorical, others literal, and some aren't even full visions, just brief premonitions. Those are the easiest to figure out." Nathan shook his head and did his best to recount the last two visions to Grant.

"I can't imagine things getting any better for a while, not with how dark both were," Nathan said.

"You should trust your intuition then and try to prepare yourself for the worst," Grant said. "You may want to lie low for a while. Try to recover your strength."

The windows of the house were beginning to glow with the first glints of sunrise.

Grant glanced at the light showing through. "I should go. It's harder for me to blend in during the day."

"I understand," Nathan said.

A few minutes after Grant left, Nathan rose from the floor and left the house. Despite Grant's suggestion of lying low, he needed answers and to set a plan in motion to get them.

Chapter 6

Despite the chill in the air, the midafternoon sun warmed Nathan's back as he picked his way through streets and alleyways. He tried to avoid the more crowded areas and only passed by a handful of people as he went. He could only hope none of the people he crossed would recognize him. Eventually, he came across a tall building with a service ladder that ran up the side. *I could use that as a vantage point.* The metal rungs of the service ladder chilled his palms as he climbed up. Once he reached the roof, Nathan sat to catch his breath. His chest ached from the exertion. Once the pain eased, Nathan wandered to the roof's edge and looked down. The sight sent a rush of exhilaration through his veins. Most people would have recoiled away or become dizzy and fallen. Not Nathan. A breeze swept past Nathan, lifting the ends of his golden hair, coaxing a sense of nostalgia he couldn't fully understand. Miles of city buildings stretched into the distance and eventually turned into open fields and forests.

Nathan gave himself a mental shake. He focused his attention on the streets below. A few scattered mini-people scurried about below. Patrol vehicles outnumbered civilians—nothing unusual. The day below appeared the same as any other, yet for Nathan, everything was different.

After one more glance across the city, Nathan went over to the side of the building he'd come up from.

Nathan crouched down and lowered himself back to the ladder. His blood pounded. Going down would be more difficult. His muscles strained to grip the ladder. An icy breeze sent another rush of adrenaline through Nathan. He made a steady progress down the wall. Any mis-stretch sent sharp jabs of pain through his ribs.

Once close enough to the ground, Nathan gave a light leap off the wall. Nathan panted and rubbed his sore chest. He walked away from the wall in the direction of the Predual base.

He wanted to reclaim the blueprints of his project. After that, he would ask around the black market to see if anyone knew anything about the hit on him. He hoped he'd get lucky for once and find out who it was. If he could settle the matter amicably, maybe the charges against him would be dropped. Of course, if that wasn't the case, his plan could turn fatal. Nathan rounded the corner and stopped short.

"Nathan?" Mark stumbled over to Nathan. "It really is you. Thank goodness, I wasn't sure if I would actually find you again." Mark trembled, his legs shaky from exhaustion.

Nathan grabbed Mark's shoulders to prevent him from falling. "What in the world happened? You're about to fall over."

Pain tightened Mark's expression. "I had to leave. After you left, more Union agents showed up. My mother was worried they'd kill me and told me to leave."

"Shit." Guilt burned through Nathan. *If Mark never helped me, this wouldn't have happened.*

"Look, I-I don't know what to do. I've never lived on my own before. Please...please help," Mark said.

Nathan put his own plans on hold. "I'll help you, but first I need to ask, do you have your telecom on you?"

"What? Of course."

"Let me see it."

Mark hesitated. "But why?"

"Because standard telecoms are always bugged. I don't want to be tracked," Nathan said.

Another hesitation, but Mark reached into his pocket and handed Nathan the telecom. Nathan ran a finger to the corner of the telecom. He sent a small electrical pulse into the telecom to fry the tracking device. Satisfied, Nathan handed it back to Mark.

"Where'd you learn that?" Mark asked as he tested whether the telecom still functioned.

"Some advice I picked up from another scavenger. C'mon." Nathan motioned to Mark to follow him. Mark trailed behind at a sluggish pace. Worry etched through Nathan's mind, but he needed to get them somewhere safe before Mark could rest.

At a short distance in a blackout zone, the double doors of an old cellar rested against the side of a building. As Nathan lifted the rusted chain padlock, heat ran from his fingers into the lock. Bits of molten metal scattered to sizzle in the snow. Nathan tossed what was left of the lock away and pulled the doors open.

"We're not going down there, right?" Mark asked. His shoulders sagged as if he might drop at any moment.

"I'm going to check it out. If it's abandoned, then yes," Nathan said.

Mark ground his teeth and shook his head.

"You're exhausted. Have you even rested since you left?" Nathan asked.

"No...I was up all night looking for you."

"I'll be back up in a moment."

Nathan climbed down the cellar steps. He pinched his fingers together in front of him, opened his fingers, and an orb of electrical light floated from his hand to illuminate the room. The orb hovered, shoulder height, a few feet ahead of Nathan as he examined the underground space. Old dusty shelves lined the walls, all covered in miscellaneous junk. Thick dangling cobwebs draped down from the ceiling. Random broken bits of furniture and ancient children's toys sat piled in the corners. A large, mummified rat skeleton hung off the top of one shelf. A bottom shelf near the cellar entrance held several cans of food, a score if any of it was still edible. No sign of any human activity for many years. A decent place to hide.

Nathan went back up to the surface. "It's safe. Really dusty, but I'll make some breathable space."

Mark sat on the ground, his head between his knees. The sight brought Nathan back to the memory of the multiple people who'd come to the Preduals begging to join. All of them came broken. Nathan closed his eyes to clear his head. Then he turned back to go down to the cellar to wipe out some of the dust and cobwebs.

Eventually, the cellar was clean enough to settle down in; not perfect, but at least they wouldn't choke on years' worth of grime. Mark still hadn't moved. Another glance at the dark entrance to the cellar made it click. Small, dark spaces—Mark must be claustrophobic.

"Mark, you can't just stay out here. You'll either freeze to death or get spotted by agents or muggers," Nathan said. "Our options are basements or cellars. It's too cold at night to stay above ground without heating," he said. His mind flashed back to last night. Without Grant, he would have died.

"I don't want to go down there," Mark mumbled.

"Seriously? No one will find us, and it's underground. As long as we close the doors, it'll be warmer than out here."

"It's too small," Mark said.

Heat flashed through Nathan's veins.

"Well, sorry, I couldn't find a damned mansion. I'm trying to keep us alive."

Mark flinched. Nathan averted his gaze. *That might've been too harsh.*

A few more moments passed in unmoving silence, but Mark stood up shakily. He looked down at the cellar entrance, closed his eyes, and gulped.

"Is it bigger down there?"

"Yeah, there's more space than what's visible. We'll have to work with it for now," Nathan said.

Mark shrugged as if shaking off his self-doubt, then stepped onto the old wooden steps leading into the cellar. Nathan followed closely in case Mark lost his footing. Once at the bottom, Mark paused. A shudder ran through him, but he made his way over to a corner where he sat hunched over, still wallowing in grief.

Nathan settled on the opposite side and took one of the cans of food off the shelves, deciding to inspect it. He ran a finger around the rim of the can. A high heat energy sauntered through the metal lid. An instant gag rose in Nathan's throat. The blackened contents of a thick, lumpy texture carried a foul reek. He threw the can outside to minimize the smell trapped in the cellar and took several deep breaths to remove the lingering stench from his lungs. He gathered an armful of the cans and took them outside.

After a while, Nathan found some beans that seemed more or less in their original condition. He took a small bite to test it and gained some measure of relief when the food tasted clean and untainted. He stuffed the nasty cans into a rusted tin and hoped that would be enough to keep anyone from snooping around.

Nathan reentered the cellar and handed the can of beans to Mark. He then closed the cellar doors and returned to his spot to stretch out on the floor.

"What's this?" Mark asked.

"Beans. You should eat if you can. You're shaky. Food might help."

"Shouldn't you eat too? You're still recovering from that stab wound."

Nathan gave a half-hearted shrug. He hadn't eaten since he left Mark's home. Though Nathan knew how to ignore the pains, his stomach still ached with hollow hunger.

"Look, I have some crackers with me. We can split these," Mark said.

"Alright, let's do that," Nathan agreed.

Nathan moved to sit next to Mark. Mark handed him some crackers.

"How long have you been on the streets?" Mark's question surprised Nathan.

Nathan turned to face Mark. "I don't know, around five or six years."

"What happened to your family?"

Memories of the filthy, yellow-lit apartment he grew up in rose up in Nathan's mind, he shoved them aside. He didn't like having to think about it.

"It's just... it's better I left," Nathan said.

His mind wandered back to his first morning at Mark's house. When Mark confronted him with the blue crystalline sword. He knew that weapon—probably better than Mark did.

"I'm curious about your sword. Where did you get it?"

Mark took a small, silver cube out of his pocket.

"Oh, Saber?"

Saber? Is that what he calls the Multiform? A crude name for the piece, yet Nathan couldn't help the amused grin that pulled at his lips.

"You named it Saber?"

"Don't make fun of it." Mark turned the cube between his fingers. "Why do you want to know where I got it?"

"Well, because I made it," Nathan said.

"You made it?" Mark asked, his eyes wide.

"Yeah, look here."

Nathan pointed out three delicately curved initials, N.R.C., tucked neatly in a corner of the cube.

"I recognized it right away the morning you pulled it on me. It was a requested commission I got a few years back. The guy's name was James if I remember right. He seemed like a decent guy. I don't build tech like that for just anyone."

Mark went pale and looked away. "My uncle gave it to me. He was killed not long after."

Ice formed in Nathan's gut. "Your uncle wasn't James, was he?"

"He was James." Mark's voice became quieter than before.

"I'm sorry to hear that."

A small silence fell between them.

"If you made it, why don't you have one like it?" Mark broke the silence.

"There were other things I was working on. Plus, I actually got paid to make that one. It takes time to make something like that. Living the way I have, making enough money to feed myself is priority. So, I didn't want to just squander my free time on something I've already made."

Another thought occurred to Nathan. "You said he was killed? Why?"

Mark shrugged. "I don't know exactly. My mom seemed to think the Union was involved."

Not good. Nathan struggled to suppress the shiver that threatened to run up his spine.

"Is it hard? Living on your own?" Mark asked. He yawned, clearly more relaxed than earlier.

"It can be." Nathan moved back to the other side of the room and lay down to get some rest himself.

Nathan woke to the rattle of the cellar doors being jiggled open. Cold air and sunlight spilled inside as Mark threw the doors wide. Irritation flashed through Nathan. He'd wanted to catch up on sleep. Anything to distract him from his crumbled life. Nathan clambered to his feet and followed Mark outside. He squinted against the bright morning sun.

"What's the deal?" Nathan asked.

"I'm done being in there," Mark said.

Nathan nodded. "So, what are your plans from here?"

Mark stared at the ground for a long moment. "I don't know. I don't really have a plan. I don't think I can go home. I've not seen anything about what's happened to my parents."

"I'm sorry," Nathan said.

"I thought I'd stay with you and try to find out what's going on. Maybe even find some other answers on the way," Mark said.

Nathan swallowed hard. "Are you sure?"

"What else can I do? Get captured by the Union again?"

"No, of course not. But, Mark, I'm going back to the Predual base. There're some things I need to try to get back."

"Why would you go back there?" Mark asked. "You almost died the other night. There can't be anything worth going back over."

"There is. We talked about your sword 'Saber' last night. I've made other things too and started the blueprints for other projects. I don't want those to get lost or destroyed."

Mark gaped at him for a moment.

"You said you'd been working on other things. But do you even have a plan on how to get them back?" Mark asked.

"I do actually. I know how to get in without being seen."

"I don't like this. What if we get caught? It sounds like a suicide mission."

"I'm going by myself. Just wait here. I'll come back when I'm done," Nathan said.

"No. Your plan hinges on not getting caught. If something goes wrong, you're dead."

"And you think you can come up with something better?"

"Yes, actually. I can call Lily, and I also have another friend, Gavin. They would help us. I feel like it would be safer with more people," Mark said.

Nathan gritted his teeth. He didn't like the idea of bringing a group of people into Predual territory. Sneaking through without being seen would be much more difficult.

"I'd rather put only myself in danger," Nathan said. "It'll be harder to go unnoticed with more people."

"I want to know that you're going to get out of there alive," Mark said.

"Why does it matter to you?"

Mark's fingers curled into fists. "I don't know how to survive out here. If you go and get yourself killed, then I—" Mark's words choked off.

Nathan looked away. "Fine. Call them. But they better not give us away."

Mark nodded and took out his telecom.

"Also, I don't plan to go until closer to dark. It'll be easier to not get spotted."

Nathan wiped the snow off some plywood piled against a building and sat with his arms crossed while Mark talked into his telecom. After a few minutes, Mark walked over to him.

"They should be here in the evening," Mark said.

"Alright, I'm going to get some more rest," Nathan said.

"But you just got up."

"Yeah, and I still have a hole in my ribs and need to conserve energy because I don't know where our next meal is coming from. You should too." Nathan went back down into the basement. Mark followed but stopped at the top of the stairs.

"We ate last night."

"We got lucky last night."

Nathan lay down on the basement floor knowing he wouldn't be able to sleep again. He also didn't want to parade himself around when he wasn't sure of the reason he'd been attacked. His mind churned trying to recall any recent jobs where the client may have been pissed off at him. Nothing stood out. Yet, he couldn't think of a good reason for the Union agent to show up at Mark's house. *I must have been reported to them by someone, but who and why?* Nathan wondered.

The light outside dimmed signaling sunset. Nathan got up and nudged Mark who had rejoined him in the basement. "It's almost time," Nathan said.

Mark sat up. "Lily and Gavin should be here soon then."

Nathan went up the stairs. The last rays of sunlight barely touched the tops of the city roofs. He stretched before folding his arms to his chest against the chill evening air. At the end of the alley, Nathan spotted a human figure. He shrank back against the side of the building where he would be less visible. As the person neared, it became clear that they were female.

Mark emerged from the basement. "Lily, is that you?" he called out.

"Yes." Lily quickened her pace. "I wasn't sure if I was on the right street, to be honest."

Nathan recognized Lily from when she healed him the night Summer stabbed him. Her slight frame and stature made Nathan worry that if they ran into any Preduals she would become an easy target.

"Did Mark explain to you that what we're doing is potentially very dangerous?" Nathan asked.

"I know. I can defend myself, if necessary," Lily said.

"Good. I hope we won't have to," Nathan said. He caught sight of another person entering the alley.

"Gavin, you made it," Mark said as the person neared.

Gavin stood smaller than Mark and was of slighter build. A week of sun couldn't have solved Gavin's unhealthy pastiness. "Who is it we're helping again?" Gavin asked.

"That's right, you haven't met yet," Mark said. "This is Nathan." Mark gestured toward Nathan. "Nathan, this is Gavin."

Gavin stepped closer to Nathan and looked him up and down in a way that made Nathan's skin crawl.

"This is a joke, right? You're helping this guy?" Gavin asked.

"I explained everything earlier." Mark's shoulders tensed.

Nathan took a step back from Gavin, a sour taste in his mouth. "You don't have to come. I wanted to go by myself."

"Nathan?" Mark glanced from Nathan to Gavin.

"Quit trying to start stuff, Gavin. It's so annoying." Lily stepped in between Nathan and Gavin.

"Okay, okay. I'll come along, but only to make sure he doesn't pull anything on you two," Gavin said.

Nathan's hand curled into a fist. He didn't want to be anywhere near Gavin. "I'd rather you didn't," Nathan said.

"I'm already here. What're you gonna do about it?" Gavin asked.

"Stop," Mark said. He wove past Gavin and Lily to reach Nathan. "Let's just go."

"Fine," Nathan said. He turned to lead them the quickest way to the Predual base. The tension in his back and shoulders refused to let up. He couldn't help but wonder if Gavin would act reckless on purpose.

The streets were pitch-black, making it difficult to see even a few feet ahead. Occasionally, a hint of moonlight would find its way through the thick cloud cover and briefly illuminate the cracked and shattered windows of vandalized broken buildings.

Mark staggered, as he nearly walked into Nathan who had stopped in front of him. "What's wrong?" he asked.

"Nothing." Nathan gestured ahead toward a looming building. "That's where we're going."

Mark followed as Nathan started forward again.

"He's going to get us killed." Gavin drew up next to Mark.

Nathan glanced back, a glint of worry in his eyes, he'd heard the comment. Mark paused wondering why Gavin was behaving so hostile.

They were halted by Nathan again at the building across from the Predual's hideout. A couple of Preduals passed by without seeing them. Once the Preduals were out of view, Nathan quickened the pace across the distance between the buildings. He led them to the back of the building.

"Through here," Nathan said as he slipped into the gap between the Predual's hideout and the building directly behind it.

Mark balked at the tight space, unsure if he could make himself continue. Taking a few deep breaths to brace himself, he entered the pathway. The claustrophobic space pressed in on him, as Mark followed trying to ignore the rapid rushing of his blood through his veins.

Several yards down the narrow path, Nathan stopped at the rise of a cellar door. He reached for a spot under the handles, which appeared to be the lock. A white spark formed between the lock and Nathan's fingers. A short series of clicks followed, and he pulled the door open.

"How do we know this isn't a trap? Someone might be waiting down there to kill us," Gavin said.

"Why the hell would you think that? These people tried to kill him, there's no way he'd set us up. He has no reason to," Lily said.

"She's right. None of the Preduals, besides myself, used this entrance," Nathan said.

"Why not?" Gavin's voice dripped with suspicion.

"A matter of privacy," Nathan said. "This entrance leads to my old quarters. I never let any of the other Preduals know there were two ways in. Not all of the Preduals were trustworthy."

Anxiety crawled through Mark as they stood in the narrow space. He couldn't stand being pressed against the wall any longer.

"Let's just go in," Mark said. In an effort to escape the narrow path they stood in, he pushed his way past Nathan into an even tighter stairway. The stairs ended, but the constriction of space didn't let up. Total darkness only added to the effect.

Mark's chest constricted as he rushed down the passageway only to find a dead end. A flutter of panic beat against his ribs.

"It doesn't go anywhere." Alarm spiked Mark's voice.

"Over here," Nathan's voice came from only inches away. Another spark flashed, cyan blue this time.

Mark burst through the door the moment it opened. Relief washed over him to no longer have walls pressing in on either side. Still, everything remained cloaked in shadow.

"I'll only be a few minutes," Nathan whispered.

Unable to stand the suffocating darkness anymore, Mark formed a small orb of fire in one hand, bathing the room in dim azure light. He wondered what Nathan considered worth the trip here. While he'd mentioned other projects like Saber, nothing here really seemed of much value. Just a few small clutters of junk stacked in the corners of the room.

"Mark, what are you doing?" Gavin gasped. "You can't just use magic around people we don't know."

"Shut up. He has magic too." Mark tried to keep his voice low. He glanced toward Nathan. His magic use hadn't gone unnoticed. Nathan eyed the orb of fire. Nathan nodded and gave more of a smirk than a grin before he walked to a small desk against one wall to dig through its drawers.

After several minutes, Nathan made a hand gesture toward the exit.

Mark gawked for a moment in confusion. While he was certain he'd seen Nathan gather some items together, he had no idea where they had gone.

A shudder ran through Mark as they filed back into the passageway of the exit.

Chapter 7

C hill air greeted the small group outside. Thin moonlight lit the tops of the buildings, and a few scattered patches of light found the ground. This may have been Nathan's home for several years, but now he was sneaking about like an unwelcome trespasser. A pit of sorrow clamped its way into his gut. Still, he had what he'd come for, now safely tucked away in a Spatial-box stuffed into his pocket.

"Now, that wasn't so bad," Mark said. "No one caught us, and we're well on our way back."

"We shouldn't have come in the first place." Gavin hunched his shoulders.

Nathan froze as a brief paralysis struck him. A warning of encroaching danger prickled through his nerves. "Shh," he hissed.

"You don't get to tell me what to do," Gavin said. His voice rose higher as he continued, "It would be better for everyone if you'd been dead when Mark found you."

Nathan's fingers curled with tension. "Be quiet." He kept his voice low.

Five figures appeared from around the corner ahead. Nathan picked out a few familiar voices. Summer was here. Her light voice was the easiest to recognize among the others. Nathan's heart plummeted. This was too soon.

Silence fell as both parties became aware of each other. The Preduals spent a moment to whisper among themselves and then advanced with slow caution.

Nathan's hands traveled to his hips to clasp the hilts of his sai.

"Who are you? What are you doing here?" Summer's voice cut through the night. She and the other Preduals were now close enough that their physical features could be identified. Katie and three others of Summer's favored team members stood with her.

"We were just passing through," Mark answered.

Summer's eyes locked onto Nathan's. Her intake of breath was audible. It was over.

"You! I killed you," she said. Tension sprang from her and the other Preduals.

"You should've used a bigger knife," Nathan said.

Summer reached to unsheathe a silver-and-gold-trimmed sword from her hip. "Like this one?"

Pain constricted Nathan's chest at her brash reaction. He wondered if the signs were there all along and he'd missed them, or did it only start after he'd become a wanted target.

"We don't want a fight," Lily spoke up. Her hand was clasped around a small rod she pulled from inside her coat.

"I don't know who you are, but you're with him." Summer turned her neck to look back at her team. "They're all a threat to us. We've no choice. Don't let any of them leave alive."

"What? But we didn't mean any harm," Mark said.

His words were useless. The Preduals lunged forward with Summer, drawing their weapons. Electricity and fire flashed in the night, and metal chimed in the air.

Summer came for Nathan. He knew she would. She struck out at him with her sword, aiming for the original injury she'd induced. Nathan's sai blocked the blow before it made contact. Her mouth pulled back in a grimace, eyes brimming with anger. A ball of ice grew in Nathan's chest. Not long ago, those eyes had softened for him, her hands once gentle and caring.

"How are you still alive?" she shouted.

"Why should you care? I trusted you. I trusted you with my life, but—" A lump too hard to swallow formed in Nathan's throat.

"Then you were an idiot," she sneered. One of her slashes broke past Nathan's defense to scrape his arm. In an instant, Nathan reached to catch her sword with his sai before any more damage could be inflicted. With a firm twist, Summer's sword flew from her hand and landed several feet behind Nathan.

"You're right. It was a stupid mistake. One I won't be making again," Nathan said.

A screech of rage rose from Summer's lungs as she launched herself at him, dark purple electricity crackling in her hands.

Nathan cried out as the electrical magic coursed through him. Her momentum and weight knocked him off his feet. His sai slipped from his grip to clatter across the pavement. Nathan's thoughts were becoming sluggish, but he managed to activate his own magic to nullify Summer's electric current. She continued to claw and pound against his arms and chest.

My sai. I need to get them before she pulls another knife on me. Nathan struggled and stretched to reach with one hand, holding Summer at bay with the other. He could almost reach one, just a stretch more. Just as his fingers closed on the sai's handle, Nathan's stamina dipped, deactivating his magic. The shock wave of Summer's magic that shot into his body sent a flood of nausea over him. Taking a firmer grip on the sai in his left hand, he struck out, catching Summer at the back of her head with the sai's hilt. She went limp, collapsing on top of him. Nathan rolled her off him and pushed himself to his hands and knees. His arms trembled under him as he gaped in horror.

"I'm so sorry...," Nathan gasped. He reached to touch his fingers to Summer's cheek. She would be fine, he knew. Pain pierced him to see how far their relationship had crumbled.

A scream split the air, sending a thrill of fear up Nathan's spine. He glanced in the direction the scream came from just in time to see Katie dislodge her sword from Mark's body. Mark fell as his clothes grew dark with blood. Nathan started to get up, but a female Predual he didn't know very well hurtled over to Summer and shoved him over in the process. The female Predual glared at Nathan before grabbing Summer to drag her away.

The fight's over. Nathan climbed to his feet and rushed over to where Mark lay on the ground, blood pooling under him. Lily hovered over Mark, her hands shaking. The amount of the blood still flowing meant the wound needed better pressure.

"Here, I can help," Nathan said. A profuse surge of blood poured from a deep puncture in Mark's shoulder. Nathan pressed his hands against the wound, and the flow of escaping blood slowed.

Seems Lily can handle strangers being injured, but when it's her friend, not so much. Nathan's mind flitted back to the night she'd healed him.

Nathan realized Gavin wasn't there. He glanced up from Mark and caught sight of Gavin chasing after the Preduals.

"Forget about them. We need help with Mark," Nathan called to him.

Gavin stopped his pursuit of the Preduals and stalked back toward them. "I told you, don't tell me what to do," he snarled.

Nathan looked at Lily, but she was preoccupied. A pale pink light glowed in Lily's hand over Mark while she spoke urgently into a telecom. The shine of tear streaks was visible under her eyes in the pale moonlight.

"Do you not see what's happened?" Nathan directed the question to Gavin.

"Dr. Bailey's on his way." Lily shoved the telecom into her coat pocket.

Gavin took a moment to study the situation, and his upper lip curled with anger. "This is your fault," he screamed.

Before Nathan had a chance to say anything, Gavin's heavyweight barreled into him. A shrill of shock came from Lily. Gavin's hands found their way around Nathan's throat, and his fingers pressed in hard. Panic rose in Nathan's chest as his oxygen flow cut off. The initial fear churned into frustration, which transformed into rage.

Heat shot through Nathan's limbs and gave him an unexpected spurt of strength. He flipped Gavin and himself over, slamming Gavin's back into the ground. The force loosened Gavin's grip on Nathan's neck, allowing air to rush back to his lungs. Dark, reddish blotches flashed over Nathan's sight. His hand reacted before his mind and grasped his sai.

Two quick swipes tore flesh, but Gavin's screams of pain shook Nathan out of the fight. Gavin's nails dug into Nathan's arm, and his other hand clasped the collar of Nathan's shirt. Blood oozed from two diagonally crossed jagged cuts across Gavin's chest. Not deep, but the uneven tears looked painful.

Nathan scrambled away from Gavin, chest heaving in a mixture of gasps and coughs. Nathan averted his gaze, furious that Gavin attacked him so carelessly. However, he also berated himself for injuring the moron in the heat of the moment.

Lily crouched over Mark. She'd taken Nathan's place of holding pressure to Mark's wound with one hand while her other hand still glowed with her healing magic. She stared at the two of them, mouth agape and eyes wide.

Exhaustion came back like a tidal wave. Nathan wanted to sink to the ground and burrow his face into his arms. Instead, he crawled back to Lily's side to help her with Mark. Shuffling and a pained groan behind them told Nathan that Gavin was in good enough shape to get back up. The movement was followed by a sliding clink of metal.

Lily turned her head at the sound. "Gavin put that away."

Nathan tensed. Gavin stood, clothes wet with his own blood and sword in hand. Nathan's heart lurched against his ribs. He expected the steel to bite into his flesh at any second.

Light flooded into the street, accompanied by the rumble of an engine. Gavin re-sheathed his sword, shrugged, and kicked a piece of ice across the ground. The small pickup truck came to a stop, and the driver's side door opened. The man who stepped out took brisk but hitched steps in their direction.

"Dr. Bailey," Lily called.

Dr. Bailey reached them and crouched down over Mark. "Looks like you've done well. We'll just give a couple more patches to keep him stabilized and get to the more serious stitches back at my place when we have more light."

Within a few minutes, Dr. Bailey and Lily loaded Mark up into the bed of the truck. Nathan's legs shook as he followed suit, walked through a cloud of exhaust smoke, and struggled not to cough. He found a spot next to Lily in the truck bed. Gavin already sat in the front of the vehicle.

Mark's body jerked, and his eyes blinked open. "Gah, what's going on?" He began to sit forward.

"Don't move." Lily placed a hand on his chest to push him back down. "You're hurt. We're in Dr. Bailey's truck on the way to his place."

The drive didn't last long. Dr. Bailey drove at reckless speed through the silent city. The truck stopped in front of an upper-scale Italianate house. Nathan trailed after the others as they filed into the house and wondered if he should really be inside such an elaborate home. A strong lemon-scented cleaner smell filled the air inside, making everything seem sterile. Antique knickknacks occupied much of the shelving space. Not one bit contained any dust. The furniture consisted of high-quality oak.

Mark was taken into a room down a short hallway by Lily and Dr. Bailey. Nathan pulled back one of the oak chairs to sit on, not knowing what else to do with himself. Gavin stood near the entrance to the hallway, glaring at Nathan through narrowed eyes. Nathan's gaze dropped to examine his hands, smeared with dirt and Mark's blood. Unease crawled over Nathan as he could still feel Gavin's stare.

Eventually, Dr. Bailey stepped out of the room and beckoned to Gavin. Mark was guided out by Lily, shaky and his tan skin pale. Mark sat at the table next to Nathan. Lily squeezed Mark's uninjured shoulder before returning to the room with Gavin and Dr. Bailey.

"You okay?" Nathan asked.

"Dr. Bailey and Lily think so. I'm really tired," Mark paused, closed his eyes momentarily, and took a deep breath. "Gavin won't forgive you for cutting him like that."

"I...I panicked. I was trying to stop your bleeding, and he tried to strangle me."

"Lily told me. The girl in charge, was she your ex?" Mark asked.

"Yeah."

"Has she always been like that?"

"No." Nathan's throat began to tighten again.

Lily and Dr. Bailey came out of the other room with Gavin. Gavin locked eyes with Mark and beckoned him over.

Mark stood and walked over to Gavin. "What is it?"

"We're leaving, duh," Gavin said.

Mark glanced back at Nathan.

"Not with him. Guy's dead meat. I want to talk with you," Gavin said.

"What you did almost killed me," Mark said.

"Me? I think you mean him." Gavin pointed at Nathan.

Nathan's teeth clenched as he held back his protest at the accusation. *Let's see where this goes*, Nathan decided.

"If it weren't for him, none of this would have happened. Now, come on. I'll walk you home. We can talk on the way, and everything can go back to normal," Gavin said.

"Things can't just go back to normal. I told you what happened at my house," Mark said.

"Okay, if you wanna be like that, I'll go home, and you can deal with this yourself," Gavin said.

Mark sat back down and pinched the bridge of his nose with his fingers.

"Okay then." Gavin opened the door of the house and went outside, closing the door behind himself.

"I don't know why he's acting that way," Mark said.

"It was strange, but then, I don't know him," Nathan said.

His nerves prickled with a sense of forebode, and Nathan wanted to get going before anything else happened. He forced himself out of the chair and stood up.

"What is it?" Mark asked.

"I'm going to find somewhere to stay for the night," Nathan said.

"Why? I'm sure Lily and Dr. Bailey will let us camp out here," Mark said.

Nathan paused a moment to gather himself. He didn't want to out-right discuss his visions or moments of precognition with Mark. After all, even Summer, whom he'd known most of his life, hadn't always believed him. Still, for this, he would have to shake the leaves of that conversation.

"You remember the morning that Union Recruiter showed up out-side your house?"

"Yeah, it sucked. What about it?" Mark asked.

"Remember before that happened, I tried to tell you to stay home that morning? Because I'd had a bad feeling."

"That's right, I almost forgot about that," Mark said.

"Okay, with that in mind, I want to go somewhere else because I have *that* kind of feeling," Nathan said.

"Oh." Mark frowned and stared down at the tabletop as if in thought. After a moment, Mark straightened up. "We should go then, right?"

"You don't have to come with me. You're hurt, and where I'm going, tomorrow can be dangerous," Nathan said.

Mark shook his head. "I told you I'd help you, didn't I? I'll be fine."

Nathan took a step back in shock. "You're serious?"

Mark nodded in response.

"Well, let's get going," Nathan said.

Nathan walked to the door, Mark a step behind him. Lily came out of a doorway and spoke to Mark in a hushed tone before saying bye to them both. Afterward, Nathan and Mark stepped outside back into the night.

Exhaustion tugged at Nathan's limbs. He kept the pace slow, aware that Mark must feel worse than himself. The crawling sensation of being watched followed Nathan the entire walk. He knew they couldn't walk all night, though. He led them to an abandoned department building. The front doors of the building were chain-grate locked. However, the back door hung ajar, the hinges broken. A rat ran past his feet as he stepped into the entryway. Mark gasped behind him.

Nathan held his hand out in front of him forming an orb of white light that slowly faded into green and then cyan. He entered the department building. Mark followed. Inside, the building contained broken, dirty furniture—much of which lay strewn about by past looters. Nathan and Mark stepped around the mess as they searched the place. The only other signs of life were a few more mice and rats that scurried from view.

"We should be safe here," Nathan said. He hoped he was right.

"Good." Mark brushed some dust off an old mattress next to the wall on the floor. He lay down on it and let out a sigh of relief.

Nathan did the same on another mattress a few feet away.

"Why does your magic change color?" Mark asked.

"What do you mean? It's always done that," Nathan said.

"I've never seen anyone else's magic do that. Have you?" Mark asked.

Now that Mark mentioned it, Nathan realized he hadn't ever seen anyone else's magic change color either. He'd never given it much thought and wasn't sure he should worry over it now either.

"I haven't, but I'm sure there're other people whose magic does the same," Nathan said.

"Also, I didn't see what you grabbed from your old home. What was so important?"

Nathan hesitated for several long moments. "I, um, I wanted the blueprints of a project I've been working on for several years. A different already finished project and some basic stuff."

"Project? You mean stuff like Saber? But where the hell is any of that?"

Nathan swallowed a lump of nervousness. He wasn't used to discussing his inventions.

"I almost died tonight. I want to know what I almost died for," Mark said.

"Fine." Guilt seeped into Nathan's bones at the truth of Mark's words. He reached into his pocket and curled his fingers around the small gold chest he'd placed there. He lifted it up to show Mark.

"That's it?"

Nathan shook his head no. A small green spark formed as he touched the chest's lock. A small click signaled its opening. A couple of adjustments to the chest's settings made it grow larger.

Nathan reached inside it, pulling out a wrapped bundle of papers and data drives. "These are the blueprints of the project I'm currently working on." Nathan placed them carefully back inside, not wanting any to get misplaced.

"This," Nathan closed the chest and shrank it back to a more manageable travel size, "is the project I've already finished."

Mark stared mouth agape, before shrugging off his shock. "You can fit those in that thing without crushing them? How does that even work? That spark? Did you use magic to unlock it? You had similar locks at your old home, too. I saw the sparks there, too."

"It's a Spatial-box. You can put pretty much anything in it and change the box's outward size without damaging the contents. And yeah, it unlocks with magic. Only mine, though. I could synchronize it to respond to someone else's magic, too, but for now, there's no need," Nathan said.

"But how?" Mark asked.

"Assertion of essence and will on physical reality," Nathan said. "I might not have any 'official apprenticeship,' but I've learned from a very good and, um, unusual teacher."

Mark stared at him. "What the hell do you mean by that?"

Nathan's gaze drifted away from Mark. *Have I said too much?* "Just that magic applied in the right way can be useful in creating complex technology. Look, we should get some rest, especially you."

Mark opened his mouth as if to protest but closed it again. Nathan rolled over and closed his eyes, hoping sleep would claim him soon.

January 6th, 2251

Nathan woke up before Mark the next morning. He decided not to wake him. Going to the black market could wait a few hours longer. Anxiety itched under Nathan's skin. He'd been attacked leaving the black market the last time he was there. He couldn't help but worry that he might be walking into his death. *I don't even know why I got attacked. Someone wants me dead. So much so that they reported me to the Union. What if I run into them?*

Mark stirred awake. The motion pulled Nathan out of his thoughts.

"Ugh, how late is it?" Mark asked as he sat up.

"Almost noon," Nathan said.

"I feel like my stomach's already caved in twice."

Same, Nathan thought. "Look, I need to go to the black market. I'm hoping I might find some answers there."

Mark stretched with a wince. "Will there be food?"

Nathan shrugged. "There might be, depends who's around."

"Then count me in," Mark said.

Nathan closed his eyes for a moment to gather his words. "Mark, the black market is dangerous. Even more so since someone is trying to kill me. Most people there won't care about Union warrants. But I might not walk out alive if someone's offered them money."

"Should we even go then?" Mark asked.

"I don't know where else to look," Nathan said.

"If you're sure about this, let's get going," Mark said.

Nathan wasn't, but he stood up to lead the way outside and through the city.

Shivers kept racking him, ones of fear.

By the time they reached the four-story car garage of the black market, Mark lagged several paces behind. From outside, the garage seemed empty and abandoned. Once under the roof, however, there were people, tables, fires, and echoes of chatter against cement walls.

"Stay close," Nathan said to Mark once he caught up. "You're a stranger here. The vendors get suspicious of new faces."

Nathan weaved through the garage to a stand with a flimsy cardboard sign with the word "stew" scribbled across it. Nathan knew the food would be bland and lukewarm, but the cook, Jack, could be trusted more than other people here. Nathan preferred Jack's flavorless soup over the chance of someone masking poison with potent spices.

Jack turned as Nathan and Mark neared his table. Sweat beaded Jack's brow, and his face was red from standing over his heated stew pot. "Nathan? Is that you?" he asked.

Nathan stiffened and wondered if he shouldn't have come here. "Yeah, it's me," he said.

"One of the Preduals told me you'd died," Jack said.

Nathan swallowed his unease. "As far as anyone else you talk to here is concerned, I am dead."

"Oh. Then I never saw you here," Jack said. His gaze slid to Mark. "Who's this?"

"He's a friend of mine. Say, did the Predual tell you how or why I died?" Nathan asked.

"No, they didn't say much about it. Just that you'd been found murdered in the streets," Jack said with a wave of his hand.

Nathan's stomach tightened. To hear about his own supposed murder in such a dismissive way disturbed him more than he'd thought it would. "Okay, never mind about that."

Nathan looked over at Mark, who fidgeted from one foot to another as his gaze roamed the market. "Hey, Mark," Nathan said to get Mark's attention.

Mark's fidgeting stopped. "What is it?"

"Do you have money on you? 'Cause I don't, and if you're hungry, this is the best place for that," Nathan said.

"I have a little," Mark said. He glanced at the sloppy writing of the price and pulled out a few coins. "We'll take two," he said and handed the coins to Jack.

Jack took the coins and gave Mark some change back. He then poured some soup into two flimsy paper cups and handed them to Nathan and Mark. "You two take care, alright?" Jack said.

"Thanks," Nathan said.

Nathan led Mark over to a support pillar of the garage to lean against and be out of the way while they ate.

"You didn't recover any money yesterday?" Mark asked as he dug in.

"No, the Preduals left me cleaned out. I'm lucky I got my projects back," Nathan said. "I want to talk to the last person I did work for. The night I got attacked."

"Do you think he had something to do with it?" Mark asked.

"No. He's not the type to do that kind of thing, but I'd still like to ask him about it. Maybe he heard something," Nathan said. He sat on the cement floor and took his Spatial-box out of his pocket. He opened the gold chest and took a couple of black scarves out. Nathan held one up to Mark. "Here, before we go any deeper into the market, I think we should wear these."

"Why me?" Mark asked.

"Because we're traveling together, and if we're dressed similarly, we'll draw less attention. I told you, the black market can be dangerous. We won't be the only ones trying to conceal our identities," Nathan said.

Once they'd both finished their meals, Nathan pulled the scarf on and waited for Mark to do the same. Once Mark was ready, Nathan headed to the staircase at the back of the first floor. On the second floor, Nathan spotted the lean, lanky figure of Ray and made a beeline for him.

"Ray," Nathan said to get Ray's attention.

"Nathan? You're alive?" Ray asked.

"So, you heard it too," Nathan said.

"Some of the Preduals told me you'd been murdered," Ray said.

"Anything else? Like by who or why?"

"Can't say I 'ave," Ray said. "I wondered about it myself."

He doesn't know anything. This is turning out to be pointless, Nathan thought. It might best to leave before anyone else learned he was here. Powerful energy spiked the air, and anxiety crawled under Nathan's skin. The aura of energy felt similar to being around Grant, only more sinister.

"I can tell you who it is that ordered your murder," a voice spoke behind Nathan, deep and smooth. "And I can tell you why, too."

Nathan spun around to face the person. The man wore a red-and-white, black-trimmed tunic, his hair a long, wavy brown, and he sported a dark mustache and goatee. He had to be the strangest-looking person Nathan ever encountered.

"Who are you? Why should I believe anything you say?"

An unsettling grin spread across the man's face. "You may call me...The Red Magician."

Nathan struggled to not roll his eyes and walk away. "Your real name." He added an edge to his voice.

"I haven't used it for many years. I'm not about to now."

"Fine. So, what can you tell me, and why should I believe any of it?" Nathan asked.

"Not so fast. I'll tell you, but you have to do something for me first." The strange man licked his fingers and stroked his goatee.

Nathan fought the urge to gag.

"I don't do strangers favors for empty words," Nathan said.

"It should be simple, really. After all, you already have one, no, maybe two of the items I seek?" The Red Magician leaned in too close. Nathan could smell his putrid breath and shrank back.

"Nathan, this guy's super creepy. I think we should bail," Mark whispered.

Nathan agreed with Mark. He nodded and took a step back.

"No, wait. I can sense it. You're carrying at least one, maybe two magic-infused items. I know where another one is, but I've been much too busy to fetch it myself. If you go and get it for me and turn over the items you already have, then I'll tell you who ordered your death." The Red Magician paused and grinned again. "Do we have a deal?" He extended his hand.

Nathan realized The Red Magician must be talking about the two stones that allowed Nathan to use fire and stone magic. Nathan wondered how The Red Magician would have even learned that information. Anxiousness stalled Nathan for a moment.

"No, I don't trust you." Nathan took another step away.

"No?" Heavy energy weighed down on Nathan. The Red Magician used one hand to shove Nathan backward against a support beam. A black aura surrounded The Red Magician, and an unnatural constriction gripped Nathan's limbs. He couldn't escape. "Give me the magic items you already have."

"Fuck no." *He's powerful, but he's trying to intimidate me.* "If you want magic artifacts so bad, go find your own."

"I don't feel like putting in the effort," The Red Magician said. He grabbed Nathan's left wrist, and an intense pain ignited. A small circle of blackened flesh was left behind when he let go. The constrictive energy released Nathan, and The Red Magician stepped back. "Bring me the magic item, or find out what happens next. Meet me here once you have it." The Red Magician pushed a folded piece of yellowed cloth into Nathan's hand. He then turned and walked away.

Nathan lifted his hand to inspect the damage. The skin where he'd grabbed Nathan appeared to be dead and rotted. Nathan suspected the rot would continue to spread unless The Red Magician stopped it or unless someone else could heal it.

"What the heck did he do to you?" Mark asked, his eyes wide in horror.

Nathan shook his head, still in shock. "Gave us another fucking setback..."

Nathan unfolded the cloth and glanced over it. A rough drawn map of a landscape, the location name was scribbled in the top corner. His stomach tightened. Too far to travel on foot but considered too dangerous for most to be willing to drive a scavenger out to. "C'mon, we're going to need to find a ride," Nathan told Mark.

"Hold on. A ride to where exactly?" Mark snatched the cloth out of Nathan's hand.

"Whiteteeth Valley."

"How do you know that?" Mark jabbed a finger at the map.

"That's the location described," Nathan said.

"You can read *that*?" Mark pointed at the words scrawled on the map.

"Of course. I'm not illiterate." Nathan couldn't help but take offense at the accusation.

"It's not that. It's just this shit looks like some ancient forgotten language," Mark said.

Nathan took the map back from Mark to glance over it again. Confusion swarmed his mind, but as he studied the writing a second time, it became clear that Mark was right.

Nathan sighed. "Look, we can talk about this later if you want."

Mark nodded in agreement and followed Nathan as he led them back to the stairwell.

Chapter 8

At the bottom of the old parking garage stairs, the man whom Nathan figured to be a fraud sat at his purple-clothed table. As usual, his wares consisted of jars labeled fire lizards, dragon scales, etc. Nathan turned in the opposite direction from where he set up. Mark, however, did not follow and instead went right up to the table.

Ugh, I told him to stay close. Nathan turned around to go fetch him.

"Mark, what are you doing? We don't have time for this," Nathan said. "Besides, this stuff is fake."

"Are you sure? It looks real," Mark said.

With magic and creatures such as Grant existing, Nathan supposed there could be a chance of it being real. "I don't know," Nathan admitted.

"You best believe it's real," the heavily tattooed man behind the table said. "Why don't you get a piece and try it out for yourself?"

Nathan shook his head. "I wouldn't know how to use any of this. We should go," he urged Mark.

"Right, to Whiteteeth." Mark's voice dripped with exasperation.

"Whiteteeth? Say, I lost my pet out there not long ago. She's a bit feisty, so please don't hurt her if you see her. But if you brought her back, I'd be glad to pay you for the trouble," the tattooed man said.

"We'll keep an eye out, but no guarantees," Nathan said.

"Here, take this with you." The shopkeeper shoved a bag into Mark's hands. "If she's acting up, that'll help calm her down."

"It's heavy. What is this?" Mark asked.

The tattooed man didn't answer, distracted by a woman interested in his wares.

"Come on." Nathan walked toward the other side of the garage.

Mark dragged a pace or two behind Nathan as they left. He still carried the mystery bag. Less than a minute later, Mark spoke up. "Nathan, I'm not sure that either of us can handle a far trip. I still feel awful. You're trying to hide it, but I know you're still coughing blood. I've seen you wipe it away. And now there's that curse that creep gave you."

"I'm fine," Nathan said, though his lungs burned. His exhausted body wanted nothing more than to curl up in sleep, but his head knew he needed to stabilize his life as soon as possible.

At the far back of the first floor of the parking garage, a group of about four people sat on the backs of bulky all-terrain vehicles. An aged woman wrapped in layers of thick clothes. A man nearing his fifties, evident by his grayed flecked hair. Another man, large built and in his late thirties, who sported a thick red beard. The last was a younger man, thin and spindly. They all gossiped back and forth with each other. Curious heads turned, and the conversation grew silent as Mark and Nathan approached. The older woman's brows knitted together as she glared at them.

"What you two here for? Can't you see the weather's shit?" the woman yelled over.

"Not interested in business, eh?" Nathan asked. The woman spun to face a man who sat beside her and returned to her previous conversation. "I need a driver, one who can manage tough terrain."

"How tough?" the older man asked.

"Whiteteeth Valley," Nathan said.

"He's crazy." The red-bearded man coughed.

"I enjoy challenges, but not there, not this time of year," the first man said.

"I'll go." Whispers of shock went through the drivers. A sturdily built woman with a double brunette braid appeared from behind one of the parked trucks.

"Ha, her? She'll never make it—" the young man began to say before the gray-haired man clapped a hand over his mouth.

"Watch your mouth, boy. That's Penelope. If she hears you say that, she may take your tongue as a trophy," he whispered to the young man.

Penelope strode up so that she stood next to the group of drivers. She turned her head to give them a stink eye. "So pathetic, y'all scared of a little snow. It's no wonder I've got a better reputation than the rest of y'all."

"Liar, you're just more careless," the other woman shouted.

"At least I've never gotten stuck." Penelope placed her hands on her hips.

"You little—" The older woman jumped off the back of the truck she sat on. She held a glass bottle, which must have been in the back of the truck, clenched in one hand behind her back.

"Just face it. I'm better than you ever were," Penelope said.

The woman swung the bottle at Penelope. Nathan's hand reached the sai at his belt just as quick. The thrown sai struck the bottle and shattered the glass before it could make contact.

"Enough," Nathan shouted. The two women stared at the broken glass and Nathan's sai on the ground between them.

"We'll settle this later." Penelope pointed at the woman, herself, and back to the woman. Penelope motioned for Mark and Nathan to follow her around behind the trucks. "I've got some conditions ta discuss with you two."

Nathan scooped his sai up and walked after Penelope. She stopped and leaned against a large all-terrain vehicle.

"What conditions? You're sure you can get us through Whiteteeth?" Nathan asked.

"'Course I'm sure I can get ta Whiteteeth. Still, the place is dangerous as hell. Ice cave-ins, monsters, shitty weather all year round. Most people don't come back. But I'd bet someone's paying you a hefty coin. I expect a large payment from you," Penelope said.

"How much?" Nathan asked.

"Five hundred," she said.

Horror ran through Nathan's veins. It would take months for him to make enough to pay her. "I don't have that much—"

"Four hundred. I can't go lower, so either pay it or hike," Penelope said.

It's still too much. "Okay." Reluctance made the word difficult to say. "But I won't be able to pay you until after the job's complete and I get the money for it."

"Guess that'll do," she said. "Don't you gyp me; otherwise I'll have to make the difference from the parts I'll cut off you."

"I believe it," Nathan told her.

"Nathan, I really think we should wait till tomorrow," Mark cut in.

"No. We don't need to wait," Nathan argued.

Penelope stretched her arms in front of her and locked her fingers together to crack them. "That's fine. I was gonna tell you ta meet me in the morning anyway. Gotta do some prep." She turned away and strode across the old garage.

Nathan stared after her, unsure of what to do.

"Hey," Mark said. "I was trying to tell you before. I feel awful. I think we should go see Lily. Maybe she can heal your wrist, too, then we won't even need to go to Whiteteeth."

"Do you think she can?" Nathan asked.

Mark held his palms upright. "We won't know unless we ask. Besides, didn't you just tell me earlier that you're broke?"

"I'll find a way to pay her back. It just might take a while," Nathan said.

They exited the old parking garage and entered into bright midafternoon sunlight. Mark led the way now at a slow pace. Nathan didn't mind. As Mark pointed out earlier, he, too, was drained. Yet, anxiety still managed to claw around beneath his skin. Nathan's overactive mind didn't help. It played different worse-case scenarios over and over. Thankfully, Mark kept to quiet streets where they wouldn't be noticed.

"Did you ever check what's in that bag?" Nathan wondered out loud.

Mark looked down at the bag in his hand. "No."

"Let's do that."

Mark opened the bag and turned to dry-heave. Curious, Nathan stepped over to see for himself. Large semi-dried rats filled the bag.

"Really? It's not that gross," Nathan said. He tied the bag closed again, and he took the gold chest from his pocket, enlarged the chest, found a space to fit the rat bag inside, then shrank the chest back to pocket size. "We'll hold on to it just in case. Any money to pay Penelope will be better than none. Besides, if we get desperate, I am not against eating rat. I'm not proud of it, but it's happened before."

"Ew," Mark cringed as he continued leading the way to Lily and Dr. Bailey's place. After some time, he broke the silence again. "You said you'd explain how you read that map. There's no one around, so?"

A shudder ran through Nathan. He didn't want to. He couldn't disclose everything about his ability. Mark would think him crazy. "I-I think it has to do with the magic I have. It sometimes takes me a minute to recognize whether a language is foreign or not."

"That's convenient," Mark said.

Convenient? Thinking back to multiple moments of others accusing him of lying or questioning when he'd had time to learn more than the common tongue, he couldn't share Mark's opinion.

"Hah, more like a pain in the ass," Nathan said.

January 6th, 2251

Lily sat in her study room inside Dr. Bailey's house. Outside, the sun shone brightly against the snow-layered ground. A couple of sparrows fluttered in and out of the bushes in the yard. She wished she could enjoy the same whimsical day-to-day as the birds outside. Instead, there lay stacks of bookwork for her to do nearly every day. Lily took a deep breath. The air tasted stale and provided no relief from her boredom. She wanted a break from this full-time study.

"Staring out the window won't help you finish any faster." Dr. Bailey strode into the room with a large mug of tea in one hand. He sat in a chair across from her and blew steam away from the top of his mug.

Lily enjoyed the smells of Bailey's exotic tea collection but never dared to ask to try one. She worried the taste wouldn't do the smell justice.

"Can't I just be done for the day?" she asked.

"You've been studying less than two hours," Bailey said. "You need to learn this." He reached forward to tap the open book on the table between them.

"It's not like I really *need* to," Lily argued.

Bailey narrowed his eyes and frowned. "Just because you have healing magic doesn't mean you can skip over the important stuff. Besides, your magic can only go so far. I've seen it. Anything greater than a minor injury exhausts you. Otherwise, you wouldn't have needed to call me when your friend got hurt."

"My magic stamina has improved a lot over the years," Lily recalled when healing a simple paper cut was a struggle.

"Lily, if you want to be a good doctor one day, you need to learn how to treat someone without using magic. Even if you master your magic, there may be a day when you can't use it. Especially since using magic in front of the wrong people could quickly earn you a ticket to a ride you do not want to get on."

"Ugh, I'll just do my work," Lily said, hoping Bailey's lecture was over.

Bailey took a sip of his tea, set the cup in his lap, leaned back in his chair, and closed his eyes.

Thank goodness, Lily thought. However, as she continued to shuffle through the piles of bookwork, she began to wonder about the larger picture of his words. She knew better than to use magic in front of strangers—only in front of immediate family, close friends, or other known magic wielders. Yet, no one ever explained the reason for this attitude. To most, it was just how the world worked.

"Dr. Bailey—" Lily began to ask him more, only to be interrupted by a loud snore. Bailey slept in his chair, mouth open and teacup still in his lap. Lily hadn't even noticed Bailey fall asleep in her determination to ignore him. She shrugged and went back to her worksheets. She'd ask him later.

Lily jumped at the sudden sound of knocking outside. Bailey grunted but didn't wake. Lily stood up to go check the door. She paused a moment, then unlocked and opened the front door. She was greeted by a bedraggled Mark and Nathan.

"You're back? Did something else happen?" Confusion echoed in Lily's voice. She hurried over to usher the two inside.

The hot, dry air of the house irritated Nathan's still-healing lung, and he stifled back a few coughs. Everything was just as spotless as the night before. Something bumped into Nathan's legs. He looked down to see a fat tabby cat rubbing against him. He relaxed a little and knelt to stroke the cat's back.

Lily sat Mark down to examine his shoulder injury while he told her the events of the last couple of days.

Nathan settled himself cross-legged on the floor. The cat stepped onto his lap and flopped over. Soon, a loud purr rose in the cat's throat as Nathan continued to rub its fur. He'd never kept a pet of his own, though he wished for the stability to be able to.

"That's Freddy." Dr. Bailey emerged from one of the three rooms down a short hallway. "You're the kid they're searching for, aren't you?"

Fear froze Nathan for a second. "I'll leave right away. Please don't call me in."

"I'm a doctor. I'm meant to heal, not harm. I don't ever sell out my patients."

Nathan took a deep breath as relief returned. Only this time, he couldn't suppress the coughs that racked through him. Freddy, the cat, got out of Nathan's lap and walked to another room. Dr. Bailey watched as Nathan wiped away what blood he'd hacked up.

"You didn't mention being hurt the other night," Bailey said.

"It's not bad. It happened a few days ago. I'm more worried about my hand—" Nathan said.

"Say, is he who you ran off in a hurry to help that one night?" Bailey spoke to Lily.

"Mark found him with a stab wound to the lung and called me," Lily said. "As you pointed out earlier, I can't fully heal serious injuries. So, he's still having some side effects."

Bailey looked back at Nathan. "Hm, will you let me look at it?"

"Might as well, though I think this might be a bigger problem." Nathan held his hand up to show the blackened spot on his wrist.

Bailey's eyes widened, and he motioned to Nathan to follow him. Nathan stood up but glanced over at Mark and Lily, fearful that this could be some potential trap. Neither of the two noticed his silent inquisition. *Follow your own instincts,* Nathan told himself. He followed Bailey into the room where he'd treated Mark and Gavin the night before. Various pieces of medical equipment littered the room. No doubt the wooden cabinets and drawers along two of the walls held even more. The room looked nothing like the pictures Nathan had seen of hospitals or doctors' offices. Less white and more color.

"Let's have a look at your wrist first," Bailey said. Nathan held his hand out, and Bailey grasped his arm to get a better look. Bailey shook his head with a frown and let Nathan go. "What happened to it?"

"I'm not sure. Magic of some sort." Nathan only mentioned magic because Bailey appeared aware of Lily's ability.

"The flesh is dead. I can't do anything short of amputation," Bailey said.

His heart pounded, and Nathan shook his head. He needed both hands to continue making tech. No way was he giving that up, not when he'd already worked so hard and still had so many more ideas he'd not yet had the chance to try.

"Absolutely not. I'm not losing my hand."

"Then I'll get Lily to look at it in a few minutes. Sit down. I can at least inspect the rest of the damage." Bailey pointed to a couple of chairs on the other side of the room.

Nathan sat in one of the chairs. Curiosity tugged at Nathan as he noticed what appeared to be an operating table against one wall and a cot next to the window. "Do you do everything here? In your home?"

"Yes, I do. That way, I can treat patients like yourself without having to report them to the Union," Bailey said. "How about you? I'm sure you had plans for your life before all this."

"Of course, I've done a lot of study so that someday I could live better."

Bailey inspected the stitches just under Nathan's ribs. "Looks like she did a good job on these. What's this?" He gave the stitches in Nathan's side a gentle tap.

"That happened the night before Mark called Lily out to heal me," Nathan said.

"Then who stitched it?"

"I did."

Dr. Bailey frowned as he gave Nathan a squinted stare. "By yourself?"

"Yeah..."

"How? Didn't it hurt?"

"Of course, it fucking hurt. But I didn't exactly have options at the time."

"Hm, at least that means you don't have congenital analgesia," Bailey said.

"The hell is that? And why would you think I could have it?" Nathan asked.

"It's a genetic condition. People who have it can't feel pain. Sorry, I've seen it more than a few times, and you saying you stitched your own wound concerned me. That's something someone with the condition might do without a second thought."

Bailey grabbed a tubular item with a flat, shiny end from a stand next to him. "You need to hold still for this."

"What is that?"

"It's a soft tissue scanner. I'm going to use it to check how well your lung injury has healed."

"Okay."

Bailey pressed it against the stitches in Nathan's ribs. Nathan inhaled through his teeth at the device's touch.

"Seems to be healing okay. Not as well as it should be, though. I doubt you've given yourself much time to rest, have you?"

"No, I haven't," Nathan said.

"You should. You'll end up making someone's job easy if you run yourself dead."

"I can't exactly stay in one place very long right now."

"Do you know your blood type?" Bailey changed the topic.

"No, I don't. Why?"

"Let me test it. I know you don't like the idea, but you'll probably be back over that hand. If something were to happen, such as hemorrhaging during surgery, it would be better for me to have that info already."

Nathan's stomach turned with nausea, but the more logical part of him knew he should keep his options open. Though he would try to make the Red Magician keep his word, he doubted he could trust the psycho to fix his hand.

"Go ahead and test it," Nathan said.

Bailey pricked Nathan's hand with a short needle. He then stuck the drop of blood into a small machine. "Well, shit," Bailey said after several minutes.

"What's wrong?" Nathan straightened his posture in concern.

"You're a magic user. And I've not seen your blood type before."

"That doesn't make sense. There're only so many types." Nathan never heard of such a thing, not even from Grant.

Bailey met Nathan's frightened gaze. "Among the scientific community, but not publicly, there's been reports of magic users having different proteins in both their blood and nervous systems. It can vary between individuals but is suspected to do with the kind of magic they use. Perhaps to protect the body from such potent energies running through it. There may be other less known differences in their biology, too," Bailey said.

Nathan fell silent so he could fully absorb this information.

After a moment, he spoke again. "So, how do you know this?"

The corner of Bailey's mouth twitched as he stepped away from Nathan. "You're better off keeping out of others' business. Deal with your own problems first."

The hair on the back of Nathan's neck rose at Bailey's reaction. "We're done here, right?" he asked.

"Almost." Bailey exited the room and disappeared down the hallway for several minutes. When he returned, he held a small glass bottle out to Nathan containing several tiny orange pills.

"What is this?" Nathan asked.

"A cough suppressant. You'll heal faster if you use it," Bailey said. He cast a glance at Nathan's wrist. "You're going to need your strength."

Nathan accepted the bottle, though he wondered what other secrets the old doctor kept to himself.

Nathan got up and went to the front room, where Lily held both of Mark's hands in her own. She spoke with a calm, intense gaze, though she broke off when she saw him enter.

Nathan glanced at the front door. "Are you alright? Or do you think you should stay?"

"Are you leaving?" Mark asked.

"Not yet. Lily, will you look at my wrist? Bailey can't do anything for it," Nathan said.

"What?" Lily rushed over and grabbed Nathan's hand. A pale pink light glowed to life in Lily's hand as she tried to heal the curse. A sharp pain erupted, and Nathan involuntarily yanked his hand away.

The blackened spot in his wrist grew wider in diameter. "Shit, that made it worse," Nathan said.

Lily's hands flew to cover her mouth. "I'm so sorry," she gasped.

"I have to go to Whiteteeth..." Nathan locked his gaze onto Mark's. "If Bailey lets you stay, I think you should."

"But..." Mark's voice was quiet.

Chapter 9

January 7th, 2251

Outside Dr. Bailey's house, the dark sky only held the faintest hint of blue to the east. Nathan pulled his sai from the Spatial-box to readjust them onto his belt. It was time to meet Penelope and get to Whiteteeth. Behind Nathan, the click of a door opening sounded. He glanced back, and a stone dropped into his gut. Mark closed the door and hurried across the lawn.

"Weren't you going to stay here?" Nathan said.

"I never agreed to that. I just want to help. You kinda need it," Mark said.

"You'll get yourself killed. Unlike me, you aren't being searched for, yet." Nathan braced his shoulders against the morning chill and walked toward the black market.

To Nathan's dismay, Mark continued after him. "How many times are we going to go over this? I know it's dangerous. I also know what's happened to you isn't fair. Besides, I can't just impose on Dr. Bailey and Lily. And what if something happens to you?"

"You'd be better off lying low until everything's over," Nathan said. "And if something does happen to me, just be glad it wasn't you."

"No, I have questions I need answered. I won't find them if I sit around and do nothing," Mark said.

"Fine, then just be careful," Nathan said.

As they continued through the city, Nathan worried if Mark would actually be alright. While he kept up better than yesterday, Mark still lagged a couple of paces behind. The sky above continued to brighten, and by the time they reached the old parking garage where the black market lay, the first beams of sunlight touched the tops of the buildings. Nathan went around the garage to the back. That's where Penelope would be.

Nathan rounded the corner of the building and found she wasn't there yet. With a sigh, he leaned against the garage's cement wall to wait. Mark stood next to him and tilted his head back to look up toward the sky.

"Nathan, I know you said that being able to read that map had to do with the type of magic you have or something, but what is your magic exactly? Most people I've met with magic have electricity, fire, ice, stone, or sometimes a combo of those. Then there's Lily with her healing magic. She's the only person I've met or heard of with healing magic. And well, I take it yours might also be on the obscure side?"

Nathan fidgeted, tugging at his jacket sleeve, realizing he couldn't dodge Mark's questions forever. "I have electrical magic, but you're not really asking about that one. Look, I don't always understand my own abilities. I-I sometimes have visions or premonitions, and I suspect the language thing might be related to that, but I don't know. Grant, my mentor, he says I'm a seer. But...it's okay if you don't believe me. I probably sound nuts."

"No, that...actually explains a few things," Mark said. "So, how does it work exactly? Can you control it?"

Nathan shook his head. "No, I can't. It just happens."

"Then, that morning at my house, when I thought you'd had a seizure, was that actually...?"

"Yeah, it was."

A low rumble cut through the air. The lights of a large vehicle turned onto the street. Nathan squinted through the glare and recognized Penelope's truck. She pulled the vehicle to a slow stop in front of them. A foul, bitter stench billowed from the truck. Nathan fought to hold back a few coughs as the wind blew exhaust smoke in their direction.

Penelope opened the door and stepped outside. "What? Are you sick or something?" she asked.

"Not exactly," Nathan said. "We're ready, so let's get going."

Nathan climbed into the vehicle. Inside, the ceiling hung low, and there were two front seats, but the floor stretched wide enough to lie down behind the seats. Mark climbed in after him and squeezed his way into the back. Penelope sat back into her driver's seat and launched the vehicle into drive.

January 8th

The sunlight was nearly blinding against the fields of white show. Ahead, a rise of ice stuck out of the ground. According to the map The Red Magician had given Nathan, that was where they were going. Nathan pointed it out to Penelope, and she pulled her vehicle to stop several yards away from the rise.

"Can't go further, don't want to get stuck," Penelope said.

"That's fine. I'm going to check it out." Nathan stood in the cramped cab of the vehicle, and stepped up to the front, unlatched the door, and jumped to the ground. His stiff legs protested the landing. The snow rose up to his calves and made him shiver. He stretched his limbs out as he trudged toward the rise of ice.

Snow crunched behind him, and Nathan glanced back. Mark stood up from the crouch he'd landed in.

"You're coming?" Nathan called over to him.

"I'm not going to just sit in the truck the whole time we're out here," Mark said.

Nathan nodded and continued to the mound of ice. He reached it and walked around, looking for any indication that there might be some magic artifact hidden there. Around the corner, a hole opened up in the ground, leading down into shadows. A distinct energy emanated from below.

Mark caught up with Nathan, and he stiffened at the sight. "On second thought, I think I'll stay with Penelope," he said.

Nathan took the gold chest from out of his pocket and pulled a rope from it. He drove one of his sai into the ice and tied the rope to the handle.

"That's fine," Nathan glanced at the sun's position, which hung midway across the sky. "If I'm not back by nightfall, assume something's happened to me. I'd prefer if someone came after me, but don't wait around if that's not possible."

Mark nodded. "Good luck."

Nathan cast a glance at the sai staked into the ice. "Will you or Penelope make sure that doesn't get ripped out?"

"Yeah," Mark said.

With the rope in hand, Nathan stepped into the small cave entrance and took careful steps downward along the frosted slope. The entire cave consisted only of ice. There didn't seem to be any rock or dirt. His legs strained to keep their balance on the icy path.

Wind whistled over the cave entrance, ice crunched under his feet, and his heartbeat seemed too loud. The walls held an eerie quiet that made each sound seem out of place. Each step brought Nathan closer to the vibration of energy that wafted through the air. The light in the tunnel grew dimmer the deeper he walked.

The rope Nathan brought came to its end. He took in his surroundings and dropped the rope to the icy floor. After a few more turns following the vibration of energy through the cave, Nathan stepped into a wider, open space. One wall held a circular-shaped wavering, like the distorted heat that rises off the ground on a hot day. He approached the abnormal area for a better look. The ice here was liquid, but some force kept it from freezing or running to the ground as water should. A small clear blue oval floated in the space. *That must be what I'm here for.*

Apprehensiveness kept Nathan from reaching for the small jewel. He lifted his left hand. The area of black decay was even larger than this morning. He fixed his gaze back on the jewel to memorize its position, closed his eyes, and reached out with his damaged hand. A cool tingling pricked over his skin, but no new pain. Nathan reopened his eyes and clasped his fingers around the small jewel. An icy chill ran into his veins, and he shuddered and pulled the jewel from its unnatural enclosure.

As the jewel passed the barrier, Nathan's surroundings began to blur. He still stood in the ice cave, but it was different. The container he'd pulled the jewel from didn't exist; the wall where he'd found it was nothing but solid ice. A tall, shadowy figure stood on the opposite side of the wide circular room. A few smaller, similar figures stood around the larger one, and something, no, someone else, a human, lay on the floor before them, screaming in terrible agony.

The vision faded, and Nathan gasped for breath as reality returned. Something horrible once happened here. He looked down at the jewel in his trembling hand. All over this, he realized. He considered putting the jewel back, but the sight of his damaged hand reminded him that he couldn't. He pocketed the gem and turned to go back the way he'd come.

He paused as he reached the slope. The incline he'd come down to get there looked impossibly slippery to go the other direction. Nathan's heart jolted. It would take forever to get out. The light visible through the room told him it would be nearing sunset soon. He didn't want to be left here. Nathan pulled the jewel back out from his pocket, and the same coldness ran through him. There was only one logical magic for the jewel to allow—ice.

Nathan tapped into the jewel's energy and outstretched his hand in front of him. New layers of ice formed makeshift footholds on the slope, frosted over to make them less slippery. Nathan basked in the moment of relief, then stepped up the fresh path. He would make it out before the sun went down.

Orange evening sun glare glinted off the snow when Nathan emerged from the tunnel. *Something's wrong.* Mark was no longer at the cave entrance, and the echo of shouts came from outside. Nathan pulled free the sai staked in the ice and stepped out of the cave mouth.

A pony-sized creature whose fur and feathers matched the snow skipped about Mark and Penelope. The creature pounced at Mark but was met by a wave of dark blue flame between them. The animal reared back and flailed. Its talons caught Mark, and he fell backward onto the snow. He sat on the snow, one arm wrapped to grasp the other, hunched forward as if in pain. Penelope stood a step in front of Mark. She held a sledgehammer with both hands, swung it forward, and caught the beast in the rump. The creature yelped and skittered a distance away.

Nathan paused and stared for a moment. The creature resembled an animal in children's stories. Catlike hind paws, a tufted tail, wings, birdlike front feet, and head. A griffin. Nathan's mind flashed back to the strange man who sold mythical creature paraphernalia. The bag of rats he'd given them with the plea to bring back his pet still sat within his Spatial-box.

Nathan pulled the gold chest from his pocket and took the rat bag out. The griffin lunged at Penelope and Mark, dodged Penelope's strikes, and lashed out with its talons.

Nathan lifted his palm outward. A spark of electricity formed in his hand and grew into a large crackling orb. He tossed the ball of electricity forward, and it landed between the griffin and Mark and Penelope. All three of them lurched away from the sparks.

The griffin turned its attention to Nathan, let out a shriek, and rushed across the snow. Nathan grabbed one of the rats from the bag. The griffin barreled into him and pinned him into the snow. He released a pulse wave of electricity to stun the beast. The griffin froze for a moment, and Nathan took the chance to scramble out from under it and threw the dead rat between himself and the griffin.

The creature shook its feathers out and pounced on the rat. Nathan threw another rat in front of the griffin and took a cautionary step closer to the animal. Food kept the griffin too occupied to care. A glimpse of something shiny on the animal's neck caught Nathan's eye. He reached out, and the griffin snapped its beak at him. Nathan jerked his hand back. The griffin had already finished both rats. He gave it another and successfully grabbed the shiny thing on its neck, a collar. *This is definitely that guy's pet.* The word "Pumpkin" was engraved on the name tag. Pumpkin the griffin bunted its head against Nathan's chest and made a low crooning noise.

Alarm shot through Nathan as a yell cut through the air. Penelope held her hammer ready as she ran toward the griffin and him. The griffin lifted its wings, spun with a squawk, and knocked Nathan over.

"Wait, stop," Nathan yelled.

Penelope came to a stop. The griffin stood in front of Nathan, its wings held out and its neck feathers standing up.

"Don't hurt it." Nathan stood and brushed snow from himself. "Someone asked us to bring it back."

"You fucking serious right now?" Penelope asked. "That thing attacked us. Your friend's all clawed up."

Nathan's gaze traveled back to Mark, who was sitting on the ground. "I am serious. There's room in your truck's trailer."

"You're both demons. Y'know, I'd never agreed to business with you if I'd known you were fucking demons," Penelope said.

We both used magic, of course... "Well, you did agree. So, what will it be? Ditch us out here, gain nothing, or take us back and get your pay?" Nathan asked.

Penelope rocked on her heels and bared her teeth. "Effing dick, I got room in the trailer. Could've told me you were catching some oversized varmint."

Penelope trudged back toward her truck. Nathan followed and encouraged the griffin with the rats. Penelope yanked the door of the truck trailer open. Nathan threw a couple of dead rats inside and let the griffin leap after them. Penelope pulled the door shut and locked it. The trailer rocked as the griffin banged around inside.

Free of the beast, Nathan ran to Mark. Mark hugged his arms around himself, patches of blood staining his ripped shirt.

"Mark? How bad is it?" Nathan asked.

Mark's gaze lifted, his eyes tired and glazed. "I...don't know."

"Let me see." Nathan reached to move Mark's hand out of the way.

"You're not Lily." Mark refused to move his hand.

"No, I'm not, but I'm the best you've got at the moment," Nathan said. "Unless you'd prefer Penelope."

Mark let one hand drop from the wound. Blood beaded from three shallow scratches that ran across his ribs. Relief rushed over Nathan to see that the damage was minimal. He dug into his Spatial-box and found an antiseptic and his supplies for treating wounds.

"This isn't bad. It's practically done bleeding," Nathan said. "It just needs to be cleaned and wrapped to make sure it doesn't get infected."

"A-as long you're sure...," Mark gasped.

Nathan rubbed the antiseptic over the scratches.

Mark inhaled through his teeth and scooted backward away from Nathan. "That hurt."

"Well, no shit," Nathan said. He finished cleaning the scratches and took out some tape and gauze to cover the injury.

Nathan helped pull Mark back to his feet and guided him into Penelope's truck. Mark clambered into the back and lay down.

"We're going back ta the city, right?" Penelope asked.

"Yes." Nathan inspected his damaged wrist. The rot reached the bottom of his palm now.

Penelope reached to turn the truck on, but the engine choked and stalled.

"That didn't sound good," Nathan said.

"Fuck." Penelope stomped her feet on the floorboards before she jumped out of the truck to lift the lid.

Nathan leaned back against the truck seat and sighed. He knew little to nothing about repairing vehicles and would only get in Penelope's way if he tried. Several minutes slid past as Penelope beat around the engine outside.

Mark sat up in the back. He seemed more alert as if the shock from earlier had worn off. "She's having issues with the truck?"

"Seems like it."

"I might be able to help. I normally did the repairs on my parents' car," Mark said.

"Really?" Nathan recalled Mark mentioning he had a special interest in cars before.

Mark nodded, pushing past Nathan to go outside. Eventually, Penelope and Mark climbed back into the truck, and Penelope successfully turned the truck's engine.

"I hate to say it, but you were actually useful," Penelope told Mark.

"Enough for you to lower your price a little?" Mark pressed the question.

"I'll consider it," Penelope said. "Depending on how well the truck continues to run on the way back."

Chapter 10

January 9th

    After a long day of driving, the sun hung low over the city streets when they reached the black-market garage. Nathan twisted in his seat to wake Mark. Mark sat up, though he was clearly still groggy.

Penelope clicked the vehicle into park. "I'll be waiting here for my payment. Better come back with it. Otherwise I'll run you down," she said.

"You've made that clear," Nathan said. He shuddered on the inside. The griffin's owner never told him how much they'd pay for bringing back his pet, and The Red Magician wouldn't pay him. Nathan would have to avoid Penelope for a few months while he tried to make enough to pay her.

Nathan climbed out of the vehicle and went to the trailer where Pumpkin, the griffin, slept curled against the far wall. He undid the latch but held the door closed, Pumpkin's head shot up. It stood up, and the trailer shook from the animal's weight. Nathan dropped a rat into the trailer, which Pumpkin gobbled up. He pulled the rope out of his Spatial-box and cracked the door open an inch. When Pumpkin didn't try to press through, he opened the door wider and reached for Pumpkin's collar. Nathan looped the rope around the collar and encouraged the griffin to follow him. The dead rats helped keep Pumpkin's attention.

Nathan led the griffin toward the black market entrance but stopped before he entered. Leading such a large and strange animal around would attract too much unwanted attention. He glanced at Mark, who stood near Penelope's truck.

"Hey, Mark. Remember the guy who gave us the rat bag?" Nathan asked.

"The guy with all those tattoos? Yeah," Mark said.

"Can you find him and bring him here?"

"By myself?"

"You'd rather hold the griffin? I don't want to cause a scene."

"No way, I think it likes you better than me. I'll be back." Mark turned and disappeared under the parking garage overhang.

Nathan ruffled Pumpkin's thick, soft feathers with one hand while he waited for Mark to return. Not much time passed before Pumpkin tugged against the rope tied to her collar and let out a squawk. Mark came around the corner of the market's entrance, with the tattooed trader following close behind. Pumpkin, the griffin, bounced like an excited puppy and snatched the rope from Nathan's hands as it rushed forward. Pumpkin jumped on its owner, knocking him down, and covered the man in licks.

The man laughed and pushed the griffin off himself. "You brought her back. I can't believe it," the man said and got up back to his feet. The man walked over to Nathan. "I suppose I did promise to pay you for the trouble," he said and handed over a small pouch.

"Thank you. It's a very...unusual pet. Where did you find it?" Nathan asked.

"In the mountains. Pumpkin's the only one I've ever seen," the man said. The griffin's owner untied the rope from its collar and handed it back to Nathan. He encouraged the griffin to follow him down an alleyway away from the black market.

Nathan counted the money in the pouch given to him. One seventy-five, more than he'd expected, but less than half of what he owed Penelope. He made his way to Penelope to hand her the payment.

She counted the amount herself. Her eyes hardened, and her brow furrowed. Penelope pulled a long dagger from her belt and lifted the blade so the point poked against Nathan's throat. "This isn't even half of what we agreed on," she snarled.

Nathan flinched and gritted his teeth. "I'll get the rest. Put your knife down," his voice came calm despite the rush of blood through his veins.

Penelope pulled the dagger back. "Fine. You better."

Nathan nodded and turned to go inside the old parking garage, waving Mark to follow him. The walls echoed with various chatter. Nathan's left hand ached and tingled with cold. He glanced down at the blackened skin and grimaced. He hoped the Red Magician would uphold his end of the deal. The memory of Dr. Bailey's suggestion of amputation rang through Nathan's mind and sent a shudder down his spine.

The number of people in the black market was larger than usual. Some foreboding in the back of his consciousness set Nathan on edge. A flash of obnoxious red from across the room caught his attention. The Red Magician.

Nathan strode toward the man. He kept his shoulders back despite the tension that tugged at each muscle. The Red Magician turned as Nathan neared him.

The Red Magician's face lit up when he caught sight of Nathan. "You're back and seem to have what I asked for. Now, give it to me."

Nathan stood still for a moment, then lifted his blackened hand. "You did this. You said you would fix it. You know I have the items, so fix this before I hand them over."

The Red Magician scoffed. "You're in no position to bargain with me. Give me the artifacts, or I'll kill you right here."

Nathan knew he meant it. A wave of tiredness washed over him as he acknowledged defeat. Nathan took two of the stones from his Spatial-box.

"The third?" The Red Magician pressed.

Nathan flashed the Red Magician an irritated glance and reached into his pocket, where he'd placed the newest artifact. He pulled the last stone into the open, and a high-pitched vibration of energy pierced the air. The Red Magician reached for the stones but pulled his hand back as a connective shock wave cut through all three artifacts.

A dark haze engulfed the stones, and they lifted out of Nathan's hand into the air, where they converged into one shadowy, liquid mass. A pulse of energy shot up Nathan's arm and traveled through every nerve in his body. Dazed, he staggered, and struggled to figure out what happened through bleared vision.

"Nathan, are you okay?" Mark grabbed Nathan's upper arm and opposite shoulder as Nathan nearly lost his balance.

After a few deep breaths, Nathan's vision cleared. The magic stones were gone, but a solid black bracelet encircled his damaged left arm. The Red Magician stared at Nathan, his mouth agape and eyes blazing with fury.

Something else was coming. Nathan could sense a heaviness in the air.

A screech of anger rose from The Red Magician, and he launched himself at Nathan. He shoved Mark aside and tackled Nathan to the ground. The Red Magician clung to the black bracelet and fought to pull it off. The bracelet slid as far as his wrist but no further. Still in shock, Nathan attempted to kick the agitated man away.

The Red Magician shrieked as Nathan broke away and scrambled to his feet. There was a scrape of metal. Nathan didn't have time to react before pain stung at his elbow. Horror twisted his guts as his damaged, blackened hand hit the ground. So much for a safe amputation from Dr. Bailey. Yet, even as he stared in dismay, orange embers appeared on the cut end of the severed arm and burned. His bleeding stopped, and to his astonishment, his arm reformed as the dead arm burned away. The black bracelet returned with the restoration of his hand, which came back healthy, no longer cursed.

Nathan's relief didn't last as the heaviness in the air grew. A dark mass that sucked energy into itself was now visible behind The Red Magician. The Red Magician glanced back at the mass and gave Nathan a hostile glare. "I'll find you again, and when I do, I'm going to rip your magic from you," The Red Magician snarled. The Red Magician bolted to the parking garage's exit.

Nathan turned his attention back to the forming mass, energy drained from anything and everyone in its range. He didn't know what it was, but his best guesses were some type of vacuum or black hole.

"What is that?" Mark asked.

No sooner than Mark spoke, the mass froze its process of gathering energy. An eerie stillness swept over the area, followed by an explosive pulse wave that echoed out. Nathan's head filled with ringing, and his vision went dark.

Consciousness resurfaced at the edges of Nathan's mind, and he slowly pushed himself up to his hands and knees. The dusty floor swayed under him, and he lowered himself back down to rest his head on his hands. Not daring to move again until the ground beneath him became steady. When it finally did, he sat up cautiously.

Unsure of how much time had passed, his thoughts shot to Mark who had been next to him before the blast or — whatever that was. His breath caught as he glanced around. Grant was there, a few feet away, kneeling next to Mark's limp frame.

"I-is he okay?"

Grant's covered head lifted. "He's still alive. Not everyone is so lucky."

"What was that?" Nathan asked. The heavy energy still emanated from somewhere. He could see the people in the building were either lying on the ground motionless or, like himself, just woken up. Screams carried from outside, muffled by the cement walls.

"I knew those stones were sinister," Grant spoke under his breath. "Nathan, that...thing...that's materialized—it's a fragment of Pontec, the original wielder of that bracelet. That phantom must have been released when the bracelet reformed."

Nathan cringed in instinct at the wet crunches he imagined for crushed skulls and snapped limbs. "Can anything be done?"

"The apparition's form is unstable. It may lose its foothold here if it's disrupted with enough energy."

Nathan clambered to his feet. "You mean with magic then?"

Grant's gloved hand clawed at the cement floor, and his head lifted. "Strong enough magic could work. That bracelet attached itself to you. If I were you, I'd take advantage of it."

Nathan lifted the bracelet to examine it closer. Cloudy, iridescent colors flowed in sluggish veins within the smooth black bracelet. The bracelet left a full-inch gap between itself and his flesh. He wrapped his fingers around the bracelet and tugged it down his arm. The bracelet stopped at his wrist. Nathan pulled a little harder but with no success.

I'll figure it out later. Nathan set forward to follow Pontec's trail of destruction, streets spattered and wet with fresh blood. The sides of buildings crumbled into piles of red brick scattered on the streets. Even the ground lay ripped and shredded with deep gouges through the sidewalks.

Nathan stopped in front of a corpse, the flesh rent by magic, and lifeblood spilled into the ground. Coldness snaked through his limbs, and he swallowed hard. *I can't do this.* He closed his eyes for a moment to pull his nerves together. *But...I'm going to be killed anyway. Besides, I'm partially responsible for this,* he reminded himself. If he'd ignored, or maybe ran from the Red Magician from the start this wouldn't have happened.

He stepped around the corpse into the alleyway and onto the street beyond. A tall, gray-skinned creature with pronounced sharp-fanged teeth wreaked havoc on everything it neared. Black energy spilled from Pontec's hands. It hovered gaseous in the air, the edges turning a faint purple. The magic tore matter from everything it neared. The energy appeared as if it were a controlled black hole.

Nathan gulped the air but steeled himself to fight. Warm energy flowed through him as his magic activated. The black bracelet gave a faint purple glow. He created a sphere of electricity. Then he hurled the magic to strike Pontec. The sphere hit but seemed to do little to no damage. Pontec turned to search for his attacker. *That was a bad idea.*

Pontec's head turned to face Nathan. He dropped to the ground as a tendril of magic shot through the air. The magic hit the wall above him. He covered his head as hunks of brick and cement showered down on him. Pontec strode over to him. Nathan sent a current of fire mixed with electricity at the being. The apparition wavered for a moment like a disrupted electronic screen. A mixture of hope and panic fluttered in Nathan's chest. His attack did something, but it wasn't enough.

Nathan swiped the air aimlessly as a force collided into him. Wind whipped around him as he got thrown down the street. He hit the ground and tumbled into a pile of rubble. Nathan raised a hand to his brow in an attempt to reorient himself. Shaking, he forced himself back to his feet. Somehow, he'd avoided being shredded to pieces. The black bracelet glowed with a vibrant purple light.

Pontec extended his hand. An ethereal black whip with long, thick spikes materialized in his grip. A faint, prickling, tingle ran through Nathan's body. His immediate world dimmed as some invisible thread pulled his mind elsewhere into a vision. *No, not now. This can't happen now.*

Nathan found himself standing in a broken city of stone. The creature Pontec was here, only more solid. People, humans, and other creatures who did not appear to be humans fought Pontec. They appeared more experienced and stronger than Nathan knew himself to be. One by one, each of them fell the instant the screeching, black-spiked whip so much as brushed them. This wasn't the Pontec released from the bracelet, this was a past version of the creature from it still lived.

"Nathan, move," Mark's voice shouted.

A burst of blue light flashed, cutting through the vision. Hot pain sent Nathan staggering to fall sideways to the ground. The whip struck where he'd stood moments before.

Nathan struggled back to his feet, winded from the electrical attack. Everything ached, and his body trembled. Heat and cold seared his veins. Nathan caught a glimpse of Mark several yards away. Unable to reach him, Mark must have thrown the electricity to keep Nathan from being struck down by the phantom creature.

He returned his attention to Pontec.

Even though this form of Pontec wasn't the same as he'd just witnessed in his vision, he now worried if it was possible to win against the phantom.

He willed another surge of energy to rise through him, gathering the magic into a tight sphere in his hands. Releasing the knot of mixed magic at Pontec, its form wavered again. This time taking longer to stabilize. Mark bridged the distance between them.

"Nathan, we should go," Mark said.

"No, I need to stop this thing."

Nathan rushed forward and sent out multiple charged bursts of magic. Each hit destabilized Pontec little by little. He dodged to the side as Pontec swiped the whip at him again. Tiredness dragged at Nathan's limbs. A beam of dark blue electric and fire magic struck at Pontec, Mark's magic. Nathan briefly glanced back at his friend, grateful for the help.

Nathan stopped and raised his hand above him. An orb of magic formed in the air, four magics twisting together inside. He summoned the rest of his strength into the orb and threw it into Pontec.

An ear-splitting screech ripped through the air, and Pontec's form dissolved into shadowy mist.

Weakness gripped Nathan's body. He'd used too much magic at once. His hands burned as they connected with asphalt. The ground seemed to move under him. His arms shook from his own weight and gave out. Nathan closed his eyes to keep from getting sick, but the spinning sensation in his head didn't go away. The wail of many encroaching sirens battered his ears. There was a pounding of footsteps, and a hand clasped his shoulder.

"Hey, Nathan, are you okay?" Mark's voice asked.

Nathan opened his eyes and tried to push himself back up. His dizziness grew worse. "No..."

Mark tugged at Nathan's arm. "You've got to get up. We'll get caught."

Nathan forced his drained body to his hands and knees, and fought the burn of bile that rose in his throat. The sirens sounded close now. *I'm too weak.*

Nathan reached into his pocket and pulled out his Spatial-box. He met Mark's gaze the best he could through unfocused vision. "Take this and run." He shoved the gold chest into Mark's hand.

Mark gaped at Nathan, his eyes wide.

"Run now, or we'll both get caught."

"But—"

"If I die, give it to Grant. Do you understand?"

Red lights flashed into the street. Mark's eyes widened, and he bolted down the closest alleyway and disappeared from sight.

Soon, law enforcement surrounded the area. An officer pinned Nathan to the ground, their knees dug into his back as they cuffed him. A second officer helped the first one pull Nathan off the ground. Still too weak to stand on his own, he hung between them. He got shoved into the back of an SUV, where his cuffs were secured to the wall. The doors were closed, shutting out any light. A hollowness spread in his chest.

The officers' voices carried through the wall that separated them. "Who'd have thought we'd pick up Reed's lost play toy during a distress call? What do you think that thing was anyway?"

"No idea. Too bad it got killed so soon. It might have been useful for research of some sort."

"How do you think it got destroyed?"

"I'd place my bets on Clouse. He gave us zero fight, probably 'cause he spent all his energy on something else."

The engine started and drowned out the officers' voices. The vehicle lurched into movement.

The officers' comments that Nathan overheard filled his mind with more questions and frustration.

Chapter 11

C old air burned Mark's lungs as he sprinted through the alleyways. The sirens, now in the distance, reminded him of what he ran from and whom he'd left behind. He hated leaving him. He didn't know what fate might be in store for Nathan if the Union picked him up. The metal chest Nathan had given him dug into his hand. "Give it to Grant," Nathan had said, only Mark didn't know who that was.

A figure slammed into him, bringing Mark to an abrupt stop, and pressed him against a wall. Mark gasped and twisted in the person's grip but froze as several points began to dig into his flesh. When he looked up, Mark recognized the face-hidden figure that bore down on him.

"You left him." The words were spat in a deep growl that sounded too real and sent shivers down Mark's spine.

"H-he told me to. What choice did I have?" Mark stammered. "I'd have been caught too."

"He'll be killed. You could've helped him."

Mark dared to look down to see what weapon the person held to him. Mark's blood rushed cold. There was no weapon. The hand that held him was no longer gloved as earlier. Each finger ended in a thick, sharp claw. Mark's wounds recalled the griffin's talons.

"He might not be killed," Mark choked the words out as his chest grew tight.

"They *will* kill him."

"How would you know? Where were you anyway? You could have helped, too," Mark could hardly believe he still had the courage to say the words.

The person pressed Mark harder against the wall for a moment, then released him. "I was trying to mitigate some of the damage Pontec caused."

Mark's gaze traveled back to the dark, clawed hand. "What are you?"

The person grasped a leather glove from where it hung loose on his belt and slipped it back on. "Nothing you need to worry about...so long as you don't become a threat."

Mark inched further away. "A threat? I'd never... Look, there's nothing I can do. I think I should go." Mark attempted to slip around him.

"Wait." The person blocked Mark's path. "I'm not leaving Nathan in their hands."

"You think I can do anything?"

"Yes. You just need to reach him and guide him out. I'll ensure you won't get caught."

"You make it sound easy. Who are you to Nathan, again?" Mark asked.

"That's not important. Just know we have some history. You may call me Grant."

Not much to work with, but I know who Grant is now. Nathan's still alive, so I'll hold off on giving this box to Grant. "How do I know I can trust you?"

"Because Nathan values you. Therefore, should you help me rescue him, I'll do everything in my power to keep you from harm. Will you help?" Grant asked.

Mark let an uncomfortable silence linger as he considered the risk. "I will, but I'm not doing it for you. I'll do it because Nathan is my friend. You better keep your end of making sure I get out with him."

The vehicle shifted to a stop. Nathan wondered if he'd recovered enough to try to escape. He activated his magic, pulled himself as far away from the wall as possible, and melted the restraints. Another wave of exhaustion overcame him, and he panted from the effort. He sat on the floor in the dark and looked toward the doors. *There's no way I can get away in this condition.*

Nathan shielded his eyes as the back doors of the SUV opened, and light flooded over him.

"Shit. Look what he's done," one of the officers shouted. The officer reached in and grabbed Nathan hard by the arm, dragging him outside, where the officer pinned and re-cuffed him.

"This is our fault," the other officer said. "We knew he had magic and neglected to neutralize him." The officer walked over, pulled a syringe of something from a compartment in his uniform, and injected it into Nathan's arm. "Let's get him inside."

Nathan was dragged to his feet and guided inside the building. An odd prickling sensation spread from the injection site to the rest of his body. His heart pounded, cold sweat broke across his back, and nausea turned his stomach. *What the hell did they give me?* As the officers checked in, Nathan doubled to the floor and vomited.

The officer who'd rough-handled Nathan gave him a disgusted glare, lips curled. "Damn it, he's having a bad reaction. I didn't think he was a shifter."

"He's not," said the other, "Though he probably has some other type of uncommon magic to cause a reaction."

"Why's he going to holding?" the officer asked.

"Reed wants one of his agents to inspect him before any decisions are finalized," the officer who'd injected Nathan said.

The less aggressive officer finished at the computer, approached Nathan, pulled him up, and led him into a hallway with multiple doors on both sides. He opened one of the doors.

"Who's Reed? I thought all this was about—" Nathan stopped himself.

"The two men sent to capture you that you killed? This was never about them. Their deaths proved useful. They forced you into the open," the officer said.

Nathan gaped in shock for a moment. Then he shook his head, confused. "What do you mean? Why?"

The officer pushed Nathan into the room and closed the door without another word.

Fury gave him a spurt of strength. Nathan pounded his cuffed fists against the hard steel. "Why?" he screamed after the officer.

Nathan leaned against the door and let himself slide to the ground, where he sat hunched over his knees. Exhaustion and confusion clouded his mind. The men who attacked him before were really agents. His blood boiled in disgust at himself. *I should have known that. I just wanted it to be less complicated,* he admitted to himself.

At some point, Nathan lost track of time, but he'd managed to sleep and regain a little strength. He scanned the room for any possible escape. Maybe the ceiling vent, he decided. Nathan focused his attention on the cuffs around his wrists and tried to activate his magic to melt them. Nothing happened. His mind raced with panic for a moment. His memory shot back to when the officers pulled him out of the SUV and gave him the injection.

So, that's what the injection was for. To suppress my magic. His stomach turned, and a tremor he couldn't stop shook him.

The door thudded. Nathan jumped at the sound and glanced over at the steel door. The lock jiggled. Then, the door pushed open, revealing the two officers from earlier.

"Come on. Don't make me drag you out," the officer said.

Nathan got up and walked over to them. They led him through the building into an interrogation room where his cuffs were locked down to the table in front of him. The officers left the room, and Nathan sat in anxious silence while he waited for his interrogator to arrive.

Several minutes passed before a man in his early forties entered the room. "Nathaniel Rune Clouse, long time no see," the man said.

"I've never met you," Nathan said.

"Right. I'm Carson Lilton." Carson sat on the opposite side of the table. "Do you know why you're here?"

"I saw the article, but your officers gave me the impression that it's over something different. So, why am I here?"

"I'm asking questions, not you," Carson said.

"But you just—" Nathan stopped himself and gritted his teeth as Carson reached for something at his side and slammed a taser down on the table in front of Nathan.

"That's better," Carson said. "Now then, where have you been living for the last five years?"

"On the streets."

"Be more specific."

Nathan made steady eye contact with Carson. "No."

Carson grabbed the taser.

Pain exploded through Nathan, and his vision flashed. The electric current stopped, and trembling Nathan gasped to catch his breath.

"Where did you live?"

"The blackout zone," Nathan managed to say.

"I said to be specific."

Nathan flinched. "There was no address."

Carson frowned but continued, "What's your level of education?"

"I'm not sure." Nathan wondered what any of this had to do with why he was here.

"Were you apprenticed? If so, who to?"

"What does any of this matter?"

Carson turned the taser back on.

Nathan's chest heaved when it stopped, and sweat ran down his face.

"Answer the question."

"Yes...I was," Nathan's shoulders tightened as he eyed the taser.

"Then who was your teacher?"

A chill ran through him. Carson reached for the taser at Nathan's hesitation.

"Felix Gat. I think it was a nickname," Nathan lied.

"What were you trained in?"

"Various science topics."

"You were supposed to be trained by the Union. Were you aware of that?"

"No."

"Why didn't you continue your original academic path?"

"Because I didn't want to. Apprenticeships aren't mandatory."

"For you, it was," Carson said.

"No one ever told me that. Why?"

Carson clasped the taser and whacked Nathan's hand with it. Nathan jerked back against the cuffs.

"Watch yourself." Carson stood up. "My superior will decide your fate."

Nathan stared after Carson as he left the room and scraped his nails against the steel table. He closed his eyes and swallowed hard.

The minutes crept by, and Nathan started when the two guards entered. They took him back to the small cell without a word. Nathan rubbed at a burn mark from the taser close to his neck and gritted his teeth. *What's going to happen to me?* Nathan wondered and realized he was shaking again.

Sometime later, the sound of footsteps outside caught Nathan's attention.

"What do you think you're doing?" That was Carson's voice.

"Routine. Bringing prisoners their evening rations." Nathan didn't recognize the second voice.

"Don't waste resources on this one. He won't be here in the morning."

"Being transported?"

"No." There was a pause.

"Oh, I see."

Terror sent a thrill of adrenaline through Nathan's veins, and his throat tightened. *They're really going to kill me.*

January 10th

Hunched over in the small cell, Nathan examined the cold steel cuffs around his wrists. He glanced at the windowless door and wondered when they'd come to get him. *Soon now.* Tiredness ached through him.

His fingers curled into fists. All his struggle over the years for nothing, all for death. A death for undisclosed reasons.

The air stirred, and two guards stepped into the cell. "Let's go,"
one of them said.

Nathan glared at them and didn't move.

They took a position on either side of Nathan, grabbed him by
the upper arms, and dragged him to his feet and into the hallway.
Nathan's blood ran hot. Nothing mattered anymore.

He twisted out of the guard's grip and shoved one of them off-bal-
ance to the floor. Nathan slipped one hand out of the cuffs. When
the second guard reached for him, Nathan struck out with the loose
cuff as an impromptu weapon, which opened a gash in the guard's
cheek. Nathan's vision flashed as a paralyzing pain sent him to the
floor. His lungs heaved, and his hands shook as he regained his
bearings. The first guard held a taser.

"You'd best straighten out. Otherwise, you'll die before schedule,"
the guard said.

Nathan didn't care. While he'd never witnessed an execution, he'd
heard horror stories. The most common method was poison. Painful
poison to keep witnesses entertained and fearful.

The guards pulled Nathan back up, and he fought in their grip.
He got wrestled back down and found himself pressed for air under
the weight of the guards.

"What's taking so long?" Carson entered the hallway.

"He's got some fight in him," one of the guards said.

"Just sedate him and get on with it," Carson said.

"We're not supposed to sedate people before execution," the guard
said.

A crack cut the air as Carson struck the guard. "This your first day? Get this shit done already," Carson yelled, the veins in his neck visible.

A sharp prick in Nathan's arm told him the guard did as Carson instructed. Soon after, his body weakened, and his thoughts slowed into a foggy haze. The guards forced Nathan to stand and led him through the hallways. Doors lined the walls, all closed and gray.

Cooler air washed over Nathan as the guards opened the last door that led into a small amphitheater. The lights shone too bright overhead. A small crowd of morbid observers had gathered near the front. Despite the sedative, his guts squirmed, and his breath quickened.

Nothing matters... The thought bore down, and a lump of defeat formed in his throat.

A man dressed in a clean white uniform approached. The man gave Nathan a quick glance down. "That needs to come off." He pointed at the black bracelet on Nathan's left arm.

A third guard came to help remove the bracelet while Nathan's original guards held him still. The guard struggled, unable to remove the bracelet. Again, the third guard gripped and tugged at the bracelet until he panted from the effort. The guard's next attempt sent him to bounce backward on the ground.

Nathan doubted anything could dislodge the bracelet but said nothing. *Let them be frustrated. Let them fail.*

"That's enough," the man in white said. "We'll just work around it."

The guards led Nathan onto the raised platform, securing him into restraints. Nathan winced as the man in white uniform inserted a needle into his arm, followed by a second into his opposite arm. *Poison, death by poison.*

Nathan's gaze shot to travel over the crowd. Most were unknown strangers except for Summer, who stood among the crowd. She wiped her eyes as if she were crying. *Yeah, right; she cried when she tried killing me herself, too.*

"Are we ready?" the man in white asked the person in charge of the poison pump.

"Almost," the person said.

Nathan's heart jolted against his ribs. He closed his eyes and hoped he wouldn't suffer long. A shout of confusion came from the crowd and shook Nathan out of his thoughts. Fire—a dark blue magic made fire tore along the platform and blocked his view of the crowd.

"Kill him, now," the man in white shouted.

Liquid ran up the tubes attached to the needles in Nathan's arms. Pain burned into his veins. Nathan gritted his teeth to hold back the cry of hurt that rose within him.

A section in the wall of fire lowered, and someone with his face wrapped in scarves jumped onto the platform. Electricity discharged from him, and the guards fell to the ground unconscious. He ran over to Nathan, pulled the needles out of his arms, and cut off one of the restraints. Nathan recognized Mark's weapon.

"Use your magic. We're getting out of here," Mark said.

"I can't...," Nathan gasped.

Through the gap in the scarf, Mark's eyes widened. He worked faster to cut Nathan free. Pain traveled like fire through Nathan, followed by...numbness. Once loose, Nathan fought through the pain that coursed within him and ran with Mark through a hallway that led to an exit. Mark pressed against the door, but it didn't budge. He placed a hand against the door, and dark blue fire cut through the door's gears. Mark urged Nathan ahead of him, and as Nathan moved forward, he found his body's reaction time had already slowed. They reached a tall wire fence. Mark melted a hole in the wire with fire. Nathan stumbled as a wave of dizziness washed over him. But Mark grabbed Nathan's arm and pulled him into the city streets.

As they reached the entrance of an alley, Nathan's body revolted, and he crumpled to the ground. Spasms ran through him, and he curled on the cold dirt as the poison took hold.

"No." Mark rushed back to Nathan. He dragged Nathan into the alley behind a putrid dumpster. Mark crouched next to Nathan and fumbled for something in his pockets. He pulled out his telecom and spoke into it. "Lily, I don't think we can make it to you. No, but I messed up. I didn't get to him in time. He's poisoned. If you can reach us, we're on 26th Street. Okay..."

"I'm sorry..." Nathan struggled to push himself back up and discovered an odd numb tingling in his arms. Fear spiked through him. *Is it too late?* Weakness ached in his muscles, and he slumped back onto the earth.

Mark placed a hand on Nathan's shoulder. "Don't move. It'll spread faster," he said.

Fast-paced footsteps came from behind them. Nathan glanced back, expecting to see a cop or agent, but it was neither.

Grant entered the alleyway, and he threw something small behind him. It hit the ground, and a wall formed to hide the alley entrance. Grant came over to them and knelt down. "They poisoned him. You were supposed to get him before this."

"It didn't work out," Mark said.

A low growl rose in Grant's throat. "I wasn't prepared for this. I don't have the proper equipment."

"Lily and Dr. Bailey are coming," Mark said.

Grant clicked a button on a device in his hand. Alarms from the direction they'd come from filled the air. "That should buy us time."

The world around Nathan grew blurred and patched. His focus shifted to the next gasp of air, each mouthful of breath more difficult than
the last. Shadows fell over his blurred vision.

Lily shoved her telecom into her small periwinkle bag as she ran through
the streets. Dr. Bailey would be several minutes behind her since she'd
only just informed him of the situation.

She reached 26th Street and turned into it. Lily froze for a moment. A
wall that never existed before blocked the opposite end of the street. Two
figures knelt over a third on the ground. Lily ran over. She recognized
Mark and Nathan, but the other person's face was hidden under a black
cloth. Lily knelt down and rolled Nathan onto his back. Nathan's frame
was bonier than she remembered, and his golden blond hair duller.

Pink light glowed from her hands as Lily reached into her senses
to learn the extent of Nathan's condition. Her stomach twisted. The
poison already held a strong grip. Unconscious, Nathan barely breathed,
and his heart rate was too weak. Lily found an injection site on his arm
and attempted to draw the poison out with her magic. A small clear drop
of the deadly liquid got pulled out from the site, but Lily doubted she
could draw out much more.

Lily gave up the attempt to pull the poison out and started chest
compressions.

"You'll save him, right?" Mark asked.

"I'm trying," Lily said. "Here, you take over. I need to get something."

Lily let Mark move to continue the chest compressions while she dug
into her bag. She took out a syringe of atropine and injected Nathan. She
hoped that it could stabilize his heart until Dr. Bailey arrived.

Dr. Bailey pulled up at the opposite end of the street and got out of his pickup, limping over to them. "Dammit, Lily, interrupting an execution. Are you trying to get us killed?"

"You'll help, won't you?" Lily asked.

Bailey's gaze traveled to Nathan's limp form. "Of course. I'd never just leave someone to die. Let's get him into the truck."

"I'll make sure you aren't followed," the shrouded stranger said.

"If you're capable of that, it would be appreciated," Bailey said.

Bailey helped Mark lift Nathan to carry him to the truck. Once they were ready and loaded, Lily braced herself against the side of the truck bed beside Nathan as Bailey hit the gas to race through the city.

Chapter 12

T he warm glow of sunlight coaxed Nathan's mind back into awareness. Light flowed into the small, sterile room through a tall, floral-curtained window next to him. He lifted a hand to his face. Something wasn't right. He levered himself on a shaky elbow and pulled off an oxygen mask. A tug in his arm that restricted his reach drew his attention to an IV line placed in it. His throat burned, and his mouth was dry. With caution, Nathan sat up. Every muscle ached and protested. He put his feet over the edge of the bed and paused to catch his breath as dizziness filled his head.

"Don't you try to get up," a gruff voice said.

Nathan turned his head to see Bailey stand up from a chair on the other side of the room. Wooden cabinets lined the walls, and an operating table lay against the wall farthest from Bailey. *I'm in one of Bailey's patient rooms.*

"Hey." Nathan's voice came out much quieter and weaker than he expected.

Dr. Bailey walked over to stand next to Nathan. "You're talking. That's an improvement."

"How long...?" Nathan tried to ask, but his voice faltered.

"Almost a whole day. You came to yesterday evening, but this is the first you've been coherent," Bailey said. "You're really damn lucky to have survived CE12 poisoning. Plus, from what I can tell, you shouldn't have any permanent damage from it either."

Bailey reached over to a table next to the bed and grabbed a paper off it. He handed the paper to Nathan. "I found this record and printed it out. Who knows, maybe it'll help you out."

Nathan's gaze dropped down to the piece of paper—a birth record, his own birth record. The information looked correct despite not being original. Nathaniel Rune Clouse, 01/11/2233, mother Loretta Clouse, father Horace Clouse, location Valen City, Union Building X. Nathan's breath caught in his throat—Union Building X, not a hospital. That must have been what Bailey meant. Ice ran into his veins.

"Your hand seems better, but what the heck is this?" Bailey tapped the black bracelet on Nathan's arm. "It doesn't seem to come off."

"I think it's permanent. It doesn't hurt or anything, though."

"As long as you're okay with it." Bailey turned away and walked to the door. "I'll let your friends know you're awake, but don't get up. You need rest."

"Okay," Nathan said.

He sat in silence for the next several minutes unable to decide what to make of everything just yet. His thoughts kept returning to his capture and questioning, wishing that he'd learned something more useful from it.

"Nathan, I'm glad you're up. Are you okay?" Mark entered the room.

Nathan placed the paper face down on a table next to the bed. He wanted more time to consider the document on his own. His facial muscles twitched in a half-hearted grin. "I'm alive," Nathan said. "I thought I was going to die..."

Mark's gaze darted away. "You should thank Grant. I don't think I'd have had the nerve to go through with something like that if it weren't for him. Um, this is yours." He held something out to Nathan.

Nathan stretched his hand out, and Mark placed the Spatial-box into it.

"What're you going to do now?" Mark asked.

"I'm...not sure. The Union itself wants me dead."

"The Union? Then you weren't set up?"

"Those people who initially attacked me, I found out they were agents. Everything's a lot more complicated." Nathan's gaze dropped to the gray tile floor. "I'm honestly not sure if there's any hope left for me. I...don't know what to do now."

Mark's eyes widened before he looked away. "I think...I really jumped in over my head. Excuse me." With a hesitation, Mark left the room.

Nathan grimaced and squeezed his eyes shut. *Is he done with me now?* He'd grown to enjoy Mark's company, the possibility of losing his friendship speared his chest. More footsteps at the entrance kept Nathan from plunging into more desolate thoughts.

Dr. Bailey reentered the room. "You should leave this city. Forget about why the Union wants you dead, and get out while you can," Bailey said. "It won't be easy, but that's your only chance."

"How? The next closest city is nearly two thousand miles away and also under the Union's control," Nathan said. "And I don't know anything about the place other than it exists."

"I don't know how you're going to get any place, but there's actually three cities you could try. You know about the southwest one, Endi, right?"

Nathan nodded.

"There's a closer one several hundred miles north of Endi called Opal. The third is East, in Laret, but I wouldn't recommend Laret. The population is thick with fanatics. If anyone so much as suspected you to have magic, they'd kill you."

"Why doesn't anyone talk about those places?"

"Most people just don't know. Also, there's been some disturbance this morning that could play in your favor. A Union agent has gone rogue and is stirring up a mess. Josh Black, I think. If it's not been cleaned up in the next couple days, you might consider taking advantage of it. You know slip out of the city while they've got their hands full."

"I'll think about it; thanks for letting me know." Nathan's fingers clenched as another anxiety wormed back into his mind. "Um, I got injected with something and haven't been able to use my magic."

"Hm, why don't you try now?"

Nathan stared at Bailey for a moment with uncertainty but then held his hand out in front of him to try. Energy prickled into his nerves and a small orb of white electricity formed in his palm. "Ha." Nathan breathed in relief.

"You're fine. I detected traces of the substance in your blood, but a standard dose normally wears off in twenty-four to forty-eight hours," Bailey said.

"I never knew such a thing existed. What is it?"

"The common name is ultra-negative serum. It's a chemical compound that affects a magic wielder's nervous system. It was secretly created during the Magic Panic."

"Then how did you learn about it?" Nathan asked.

"That's not important. You should be more concerned with how to get out of the city," Bailey said.

Nathan's memories turned to the events of yesterday. Grant showed up for both Pontec's appearance and to rescue him. "Is Grant here?"

"Who?" Bailey asked.

"So, he's not..."

"I'll be reorganizing some stuff. Press that if you need anything." Bailey pointed to a button on the bed stand before he left.

All his choices seemed bleak. The options left were either trying to reach a faraway city where he'd still be killed if found out, taking his chances in the freezing wilderness alone, or attempting to locate an even further away city not controlled by the Union. The latter would be the most ideal but least plausible. Unless...

Nathan's gaze traveled to the gold chest in his hands; he opened it and dug through it. He pulled out a thick notebook, a folder file of papers, a few data drives, a tangle of metals and gadgets, and a barely functional, tinkered-with wrist-style telecom. He flipped the notebook open to reassess the scribbles strewn over the pages. As he glanced at the materials available, he grimaced. Before now, he intended to finish the project after taking enough scavenging jobs to come up with the funds. Stuck, Nathan looked over the mess of papers and materials on the bed and deflated inside.

He turned away from the clutter and reached to pull the floral curtain open a few inches. The yard held several winter barren shrubs, and snow still scattered the ground. The tabby cat, Freddy, trotted across the lawn toward the house, something dangling from his mouth. The cat disappeared around the edge of the house.

Less than a minute later, Lily's voice called through the house. "Dr. Bailey, Freddy brought in another dead mouse."

"Put it outside," Bailey called back.

"I don't want to touch it."

"Fine, I'll get it."

A fleeting smile tugged at Nathan's lips over the exchange.

The sound of movement outside the room caught his attention. Lily walked to the entrance of the doorway and glanced in.

"Good, you're still awake." She sounded relieved. Lily turned into the room with something held in her hands.

Nathan's mouth watered the instant the scent reached him. Beans with some kind of meat—he couldn't remember his last meal.

"Here, you really need this." Lily handed Nathan the bowl with a fork.

"Thank you." Nathan accepted the food and finished it in under a minute.

Lily's gaze fixed on the mess of papers and wires still on the bed. "What's all this?"

"As of now? Pointless junk."

Lily crossed her arms and turned her gray-blue stare to Nathan. "Really? Then what *was* it for?"

Nathan looked away from her gaze. "Before all this, I was working on something to make travel easier. Even to far cities and overseas..." His voice grew weaker, and he rubbed at his throat.

"That doesn't exactly look like what you'd use to build a vehicle," Lily said.

"Not a vehicle, something quicker and easier to use..." Nathan fidgeted and reached to put the papers and wires back into the gold chest. "I was going to take Bailey's advice. Get out of here, but I don't have what I need..."

"Do you have money for it? Maybe if you made a list," she said.

Nathan shook his head. "No. I'm going to find Grant..."

"Not for another day or two, Dr. Bailey says."

"Did Mark leave...?"

"He's still here but upset. I think everything that's happened really shook him," Lily said. "You shouldn't have let him get involved."

"I never wanted him to. I tried to convince him to back out multiple times," Nathan said.

Lily's narrowed gaze showed she disapproved of his answer.

"Look, I think I should rest..." Really, he just wanted to be left alone for a bit.

Moonlight flooded into the window across the room. The house had been quiet for about an hour now. Unable to quiet his mind Nathan made a small orb of electricity for light. He picked up the paper Bailey had given him earlier to reexamine it. His mind flashed back to when the Union agent Carson questioned him. His stomach knotted.

"Who was I even supposed to be?" Nathan said under his breath. His fingers found the scar under his left collarbone. The physical reminder of why he would never go back to his father.

"You can't sleep either?"

Nathan started and looked up to see Mark standing just outside the doorway.

"Sorry, I saw a light and..." Mark fidgeted.

"Why are you still up? I thought you didn't want to talk to me after what I told you," Nathan said.

Mark stepped into the room. "It's not that. It's just... I'm not mad at you. Part of me just hoped I would find out why my uncle got killed."

"I hope you do find out. Though I doubt it'll be through me."

"What's that?" Mark motioned at the paper in Nathan's lap.

Nathan shook his head. "More questions I want answers to. Bailey thinks I should flee the city. I know he's right, but I think there's more I need to know."

"The Union is trying to kill you," Mark said.

"I know...but something's not right about this." Nathan grasped the paper lifting it up.

"Can I see?" Mark held his hand out.

Nathan hesitated but handed it over to him.

"Is this a birth record?"

Nathan nodded.

"Union building X. Maybe your parents were high-class agents? Got special treatment?"

"My father wasn't high-class anything." Nathan's teeth clenched.

"Your mother?"

"I'm not sure. She got taken when I was six."

"Taken? Where?"

Nathan looked away his chest constricting as his memory shot back to the day his mother was taken. She'd screamed as those men dragged her out of the house, and there had been nothing he could do, but watch in horror.

"I don't think it has anything to do with this."

"But what if it does? Where was she taken?"

Nathan's fingers grasped tight onto the edge of the blanket. "Just drop it, okay?"

Mark lifted his hands and took a step back. "Okay, sorry."

"I just want to know what's happening. Why I ever got pulled into this, or my family anyway. It's stupid and I probably shouldn't, but what I learned doesn't feel complete," Nathan said.

Mark nodded. "I'm going to stay with Lily and Dr. Bailey a little longer. I finally heard from my mom. She and my dad are okay for now, but she's not sure if I can go back yet. I'm going to need to come up with some excuse about why I've been gone. You should take Dr. Bailey's advice and leave the city. You'll be killed if you stick around."

"I'm glad your parents are okay. Will you be able to go back to your old life?" Nathan wondered out loud.

"I have to try," Mark said.

Nathan's gaze drifted to the floor. "I hope you can."

Chapter 13

January 13th

Midday light glared through the window spreading across the carpet of Bailey's living room. Nathan finished his breakfast and walked to the front door. A mild ache still lingered in Nathan's muscles from the poison as he pulled his boots on. The events of the last several days flashed through his mind. *I'm still alive. That means I can still find a way to get through this, can't I?* A heavy weight settled in Nathan's chest as he stared at the door and wondered where to start.

"You're leaving today?" Lily came up behind him.

"I was planning to."

"You're still weak. I think you should hold off."

"No, the sooner I get going, the better." As far as he knew the Union was still searching for their rogue agent, and he wanted to take the opportunity to hopefully move unnoticed. Hopefully he'd be able to find Grant and ask for his help. He paused at the door having a sudden realization. His jacket had been confiscated by the Union before his botched execution. Nathan's fingers curled, nothing he could do about it right now. Bracing himself he opened the door and stepped outside.

"Hey, wait."

He stopped to look back at Lily's call.

She chased after him and pushed a worn fleece jacket into his hands. "Are you nuts? You'll freeze without this."

"You're sure I can have it?"

"It's an older one of Dr. Bailey's. He doesn't use it anymore. I'll doubt he'll even notice it's missing."

"Thank you, this'll help a lot." Nathan pulled the jacket on. It was too large for his thin frame, but it's warmth sent a shudder of relief through him.

"I can walk with you for a while. Dr. Bailey asked me to pick up some supplies," Lily said.

"Alright, I was going to look for Grant," Nathan said.

"I thought you wanted to leave the city," Lily said.

"I do, but I need to talk to him. I think I'm going to need help getting the materials for the project I've been working on," Nathan said.

Lily crossed her arms. "You're worried about that, of all things? You never told me what this project is anyway."

Nathan looked down and scraped the snow with his shoe. "I, um, I'm making a teleporter."

"Really?" Lily walked down the last few steps.

Nathan nodded.

"I'll be impressed if you can pull it off," Lily said.

Nathan fell into step beside Lily on the cracked street. "Bailey's kind of secretive, isn't he?"

Lily shrugged. Her gaze fixed on the ice-patched ground. "He doesn't talk about his past much. He's never told me what he used to do."

"He wasn't always a doctor?"

"I'm not sure. He opened the clinic about fifteen years ago and took me in seven years ago. He doesn't talk about his life before opening the clinic, though. I think he must have been through something awful. He's shut me down every time I've tried to ask, especially if he's in one of his moods."

"Moods? What do you mean by that?" Nathan couldn't help but think back to his own childhood.

"Just times when he wants to be left alone. Even though there's something bothering him, he just won't open up about it," Lily said. She shook her head. "Don't take it the wrong way, though. Dr. Bailey has been very good to me. He's almost like a second father to me."

In the distance, a horn blared, followed by angry shouting. Nathan and Lily both stopped, but the noise faded away. Sure that they weren't going to walk into danger, Nathan and Lily continued forward.

"Seven years, did you start your apprenticeship early?"

"No, I started my apprenticeship at twelve, like everyone else. Dr. Bailey is my godfather."

"I'm sorry."

"Don't be. I've been luckier than most who lose parents." She shot a glance at Nathan.

"My parents aren't dead. At least I'm fairly sure they aren't."

"You don't know for sure?"

"I've not seen either of them in years."

"Can I ask what happened?"

Nathan shook his head.

The clouds overhead were dark, as if it might snow again. *Just what we need, more white crap on top of this already cold shit. I hope wherever I end up is slightly warmer.*

They reached a block of abandoned buildings.

"I'm gonna split here," Nathan said and stopped.

Lily paused and turned back. "Okay, good luck. Hope you find someplace safe."

Nathan nodded. "Yeah, and hey, thanks for everything."

Lily raised her hand in a goodbye wave as she turned and walked away.

Nathan turned onto the side street. He wondered how far Grant might have gotten by now. His best bet at finding him would be going to where Grant would usually sell books and other random oddities. That was just outside of the garage where the black market used to be. Nathan winced at his last memory of the place. Torn to shreds and spattered with blood by the phantom Pontec.

A grisly thought came to his mind that maybe he could find what he needed simply by digging through the ruins—as long as there weren't still Union agents swarming around the place. He paused in his trek as he realized that if Union agents were still over there, or maybe even if they weren't anymore, Grant wouldn't have stuck around. It would be too dangerous for him.

He glanced behind himself, stalling as he tried to decide whether he should go to the ruins of the black market anyway or return to Dr. Bailey's instead and wait to see if Grant would come back.

Before he could make a decision, a thudding sound above him alerted Nathan's attention. He looked up to find the source of the sound. A man on the building lost his footing and slipped down the slanted roof. The man tumbled into a pile of garbage a few yards away. Nathan's blood pounded in his ears when he saw what the man wore. He knew that gray uniform—the same as the agents who first attacked him.

The man got up with a groan, then spotted Nathan and made eye contact with a grin.

An uncomfortable prickling ran the length of Nathan's spine as he backed away, his hands grasping onto the sai on his belt.

"So, you did survive. Damn, bastard. No wonder the UGL's so determined to bury you."

Nathan clasped his sai tighter. "The UGL?"

The man's gaze traveled to the sai and back to Nathan's face; he grinned wider but shook his head. "You don't remember me."

"Why would I remember you?"

"My partner and I used to stop by a time or two a year. You know, make sure that deadbeat hadn't killed you. I'm Josh Black." Josh walked a few steps closer to Nathan.

"You're the rogue agent," Nathan recalled Bailey mentioning that an agent bailed on the Union a couple of days earlier.

Josh nodded. "You don't know what the UGL is either? There's no time right now, but there's a database hidden on West Street. I'd guess you might have questions about what was done to you."

"What do you mean what was *done* to me?"

"Look, I gotta go." Josh stepped forward to move past Nathan through the alleyway.

Heat boiled under Nathan's skin. *He's just going to say something like and leave?* He raised his hand and focused his energy on the frozen ground in front of Josh. The iced-over ground released a faint steam as Nathan's magic melted the ice's surface.

Josh slipped on the wet surface and fell.

"What is the UGL? What do you know about me?" Nathan asked.

Josh looked back at Nathan. "You bastard."

"Are you going to answer me or not?"

"I told you, I don't have time for this." Josh's brow furrowed as he clambered back to his feet. "I killed several people breaking out of the UGL. I'm being hunted."

An empty pit opened up inside Nathan's stomach as he took in Josh's words. *That means I need to get away from Josh and hide.* He stepped back a pace, his gaze darting in search of any nearby building he could easily break inside to hide. Not that he'd be safe there if anyone noticed.

Josh took a step toward Nathan, straightening his shoulders as if sizing him up. Josh was both broader and taller than him. Nathan braced himself, well aware that he didn't have the strength for a fight, as his body still ached from the poison. Even without the lingering effects of the poison, he doubted his own underweight frame would be any match against Josh. *Why'd I have to go and provoke him?*

"You really don't know what the UGL is?" Josh asked.

Nathan gave a tense shake of his head.

"You should. It's a branch of the Union; it stands for the Union's Grand Laboratories. Doesn't ring a bell?"

"No, this is the first I've heard of it."

"I don't know why you haven't, but if you want to know anything else, you'll have to get into the West Street database. I can't hang around here right now. There're normally only one or two guards around the database on Tuesday nights. The entrance can be tricky to find—oh fuck."

Nathan flinched sideways as an enormous man's figure blocked the entrance of the alleyway.

"That's Ivan. Run." Josh fled down the alley.

Nathan followed Josh's flight, heart thundering in his chest. Only he couldn't keep up.

Josh clambered up a chain-link fence at the end of the alley. He jumped to the ground on the other side and continued his dash. Nathan reached the fence. The metal links jingled as he pulled himself up. The heavy footsteps of the huge man caught up.

Just as Nathan's hand clasped the top rung of the fence a rough hand caught his ankle. Nathan gasped holding tighter to the fence as he tried to twist himself free. The man's grip held firm.

"You're the one that escaped," Ivan said.

A strong yank broke Nathan's hold bringing him down to land hard on his back on the frozen ground. Wheezing for the air forced from his lungs he scrambled backward across snow-dusted bits of soggy cardboard and broken glass.

"They'll be glad to know I killed you too."

A metal spike-studded club rushed at Nathan. On instinct, he lifted his sai. Just in time to block the blow. Pain exploded down his arms. He gasped from the impact. Any more force would have fractured bone. *No way can I win this.* His best chance was to run.

Ivan's club swung upward. One sai flew out of Nathan's hand. Blood ran from a deep gash in his forearm. Nathan rolled across the ground and staggered to his feet before Ivan could strike again.

"Give up." Ivan raised the large, spiked club high into the air.

The air sang, and wind buffeted Nathan's face. He'd barely dodged the blow—and the next one. He lashed out with an arc of fire between them. Ivan raised an arm in defense. Not in time to avoid the singing of his eyebrows. Nathan released a blast of electricity, and Ivan staggered a step back. Nathan turned to dart for the alley's entrance.

Before he'd gotten more than a few feet away pain erupted in his back, and his legs buckled. Nathan landed on his hands and knees, racked by coughs.

Nathan attempted to send out another wave of fire. But the flame sputtered out. He didn't have the strength left to use magic. Ivan kicked him over and planted a foot on his chest. *I'm not going to die here.* Nathan tightened his grip on his remaining sai. He jammed the end into Ivan's calf.

Ivan frowned and lifted his foot, slamming it back down on Nathan's ribs. Nauseous, loud cracking filled his ears. Then came the pain, followed by panic as his body registered that he couldn't breathe. Ivan stepped back.

Nathan curled on the icy ground choking. Hot blood flooded his mouth. Spasms jerked him as his broken body fought for air.

He didn't see the last blow. The sharp pain barely registered as his vision blackened the world going silent.

A warm, gentle energy flooded Nathan, and he got up with unusual ease. Confusion tugged at him. He'd been fighting for breath only moments before, yet he seemed fine now. *Something's not right.* Just in front of him lay the limp, bloodied body of a thin, blond boy. A large man held a spiked club that dripped with crimson drops.

Is that me? I'm dead? A thrill of shock mixed with horror shot through Nathan. He lifted a hand up, visible but not fully solid. His breath quickened, though Nathan wondered how that was possible if he were dead. Ivan walked away, leaving Nathan alone with his broken body. *This can't be real. Maybe if I just...* Nathan knelt next to his own body and reached his hand out, hoping to reattach himself. To wake up injured but back to normal. His hand passed through his body. An icy tremor ran through Nathan.

"Your body's too damaged for that," a voice said.

Nathan glanced around to find who spoke but saw no one.

Heavy, invisible claws wrapped around Nathan's back. Panic spiked through Nathan, only to be subdued by a calmness he didn't think was his own. He glanced back at his body, only this time with an odd sense of detachment.

Raw energy increased around him and pulled him into a directionless free fall.

The free fall stopped. Disoriented, Nathan found himself sitting on a smooth glass-like surface. The wide shining area stretched out around him, the edges hidden by mist.

"This shouldn't have happened, Rune. You might have lived longer," the voice spoke again.

"Rune? What are you saying?" *And what the hell are you?* Nathan kept that question to himself.

The ground shifted in front of Nathan. The floor rose like formless water before transforming into an ethereal mirror. He stared at the image, shocked. The person staring back was himself, no doubt. Only this version of himself looked broken, haggard. A pair of torn gold wings sagged at the reflection's sides. A blood-soaked, gold wolfish tail wrapped around the reflection's knees, and sharp green claws scraped the ground. One of the reflection's eyes was gouged and bleeding, while the other eye glowed with green light.

Nathan flinched at the sight and reached to feel his face and back. Both seemed normal. Gingerly, he reached his hand, fingers outstretched, toward the mirror. His reflection matched the motion. The tips of his fingers touched the mirror to meet his reflection. The mirror instantly collapsed and washed away, reabsorbing into the glossy floor. A sense of loss and anger rose within him, though he didn't understand why.

A paralyzing wave of energy shot through Nathan. After it passed, he tried to recollect himself, but the ground under him seemed hazy, less solid. An uncomfortable pressure weighed on his essence. *What's happening?* Fear clutched Nathan as the world around him dissolved, and an unseen weight dragged him down.

Lily held the bag of supplies requested by Dr. Bailey under one arm as she made her way back to the clinic. Ahead, she recognized the spot where she and Nathan parted ways earlier. As she drew nearer, a huge man stepped out of that alleyway. Lily's steps faltered a moment before she pressed forward. Her stomach cramping with unease. The broad-shouldered man walked in her direction. Lily skirted to the far edge of the uneven sidewalk to give the man as much space as she could. As the man passed by her, she kept her gaze averted but could feel the crawl of the man's stare sweep over her.

Lily shuddered as the man turned into a different alleyway. With the scary man out of sight, she took a deep breath to calm herself, then noticed drops of red blood in the snow dust.

Lily followed the drops to the alleyway from which the man had exited. She looked down the alleyway, and a pit formed in her stomach. A human form lay motionless near the end of the alleyway.

She glanced back to check that she wasn't being watched. It seemed the large man hadn't stuck around.

Lily rushed to the end of the alley. Her blood ran cold when she recognized who it was. She knelt on the ground next to Nathan. He lay curled in a pool of blood, soaking into the thin layer of snow under his head. The blood had clearly come from a puncture that no longer bled. Lily placed a hand on his back and almost recoiled from the unnatural chill. Pink light glowed in her hand as she extended her senses, but she could find no breath, no heartbeat. Not even the lingering life force that sometimes clung to the dying. Her throat tightened. She was too late. Lily pulled her telecom from her pocket to call Dr. Bailey, Mark, or anyone.

Lily jumped to her feet, her heart pounding, as a dark figure approached her from behind.

"It's okay; I'm a friend," the person said, holding his hands out to show they were empty. Lily recognized this person as the same person who'd helped them rescue Nathan days earlier. For some reason, his face was still covered with a cloth.

The person approached, paused next to Nathan, and crouched down. Then lifting his head to face Lily, he said, "You have healing magic, is that right?"

"I-I, yes," Lily stammered. "But who are you exactly?"

"My name's Grant," Grant said. "Will you heal him?"

"He's dead. There's nothing I can do. I might have healing magic, but it doesn't work like that," Lily protested.

Grant pulled the black cloth from his face and let it drop over his back. Lily froze in fear. Grant's head wasn't human. Rather, it was canine like the ancient Egyptian dogs.

"Heal him anyway," Grant said.

Shaking, Lily knelt back to the ground. She wanted to run but feared this creature's reaction if she fled away. Lily extended a hand, and a pink light glowed to life as she healed the worst wound first. A blow that must have come from the attacker's spiked club, which penetrated Nathan's skull. She could also sense multiple crushed ribs.

Several minutes later, Lily finished healing the head wound but panted with exhaustion. "You can't expect me to do this. I can't, there's no point," Lily said.

"Rest, but keep going," Grant said. "I promise this isn't pointless."

"Why?"

Grant's lip curled to show sharp, pointed fangs, and Lily looked away.

After she'd recovered some of her magic, she moved on to heal the rest of Nathan's wounds. It was nightfall before Lily had fully healed the injuries dealt to Nathan.

"I told you, I can't bring him back. What do you expect me to do?" she asked.

"You've done enough," Grant said. Lily noticed a syringe filled with a pale, viscous green liquid in Grant's hand.

"What is that?" Lily asked.

Grant ignored her question and reached over to inject the liquid into Nathan's chest. Several moments passed in silence, and Grant's shoulders slouched.

Nothing's going to happen. This creature forced me to use my magic, but for what? Lily's hands tightened into fists as tears threatened to choke her.

Just then, Nathan's body jerked. His eyes fluttered open, and he took several deep gasps of breath.

Lily inhaled sharply. Her hand reached to cover her mouth. She shook her head in shock and placed her hand on Nathan's chest. She could feel his heart beating, hard and fast, as if catching up for lost time. Nathan's gaze flicked to focus on her.

"You're alive," Lily said.

Nathan raised a hand in a slow, deliberate motion as if to inspect his own hand, but he didn't say anything.

"Nathan? Is it actually you?" Lily asked.

Nathan's gaze slid back to Lily. "G-give me a moment," he spoke through chattering teeth.

Nathan lifted himself forward and raised a hand to his brow. He found the motion difficult, his body heavier than he remembered. Everything seemed vague, distant as if he wasn't fully back. His teeth chattered, and shivers shook him. "I a-actually died. What h-happened? H-how am I here?"

"I don't know. Something he did." Lily motioned to Grant, who knelt by Nathan's other side. "Do you feel okay?" Lily asked.

"I'm n-not sure. I don't hurt, but..." Nathan didn't know how to describe his disorientation.

"Something's wrong?" Lily's voice seeped with panic.

Grant's face was uncovered—unusual, especially for being out in the open and with someone else present.

"I'll tell you what I can. Come with me," Grant said.

"Don't. What the hell even is he? I don't trust him," Lily said.

Grant's ears swiveled back, and his teeth bared at Lily's comment.

"I-I think I s-should," Nathan said.

"No." Lily grabbed his arm. To anyone else, her hands were probably freezing, but Nathan welcomed their warmth.

"I'll be f-fine."

Grant unhooked the cloth he used to cover his face from off his back and draped it over Nathan's shoulders. The heat that still lingered on the fabric gave him some relief. "Can you stand?" Grant asked.

Nathan pulled himself into an upright sitting position. His head spun, and he panted from the effort. The weight of his body still heavy and awkward. He ran his fingers over the area of his head where he thought he remembered being struck. No pain, no trace of the injury, except frozen blood in his hair. Electricity pricked his nerve endings. A sense of urgency spilled over him with the premonition of encroach-ing danger.

"We need to get out of here." Nathan forced himself to his feet. Too fast. The frosted ground rose to meet him no sooner than he'd stood. Nathan stared at his hands in front of him and flexed his fingers. The movement was slower and more difficult than it should have been. *My body's not working right. Am I too cold, or is this just how I am now?* Nathan's breath hitched.

Lily placed a hand on Nathan's back. "Just be still," she said.

"No, he's right. We've been here too long," Grant said. He wrapped an arm around Nathan and pulled him off the ground.

"You can't go with him. We don't know what he is. What does he plan to gain from you?" Lily asked.

Nathan couldn't answer her, but he knew Grant held more knowledge and answers than he'd get from any human. Regardless of Lily's concerns, Nathan wanted to go with Grant.

"I-I'll be okay. I need to go with Grant," Nathan said.

Grant turned his head to look at Lily. "I apologize for frightening you."

Nathan clung to Grant for warmth and balance through the dark-ened streets. Grant stayed close to walls and kept to shadows. At one point, Nathan caught sight of two black SUVs driving in the direction they'd come from.

Nathan's thoughts shot to Lily. "I hope Lily's already left."

"I'm sure she has," Grant said.

By the time they reached a small white door in the side of a building, the moon had shifted positions across the sky. A thin strip of trees lay across from the door. *This must be at the edge of the city.*

Grant opened the door and ushered Nathan inside. A small, tidy room with two other doors visible. Pale, electronic blue light acted as the only luminance. He recognized several items to be technological but only knew the functions of a handful of them. Grant broke away from Nathan and began searching the room for something.

Still too weak to hold himself up for long, Nathan sank to the ground. The drastic temperature change stifled his breath but not the incessant shivers. His memory flitted back to the frightful moments before his death when it'd been impossible to draw even the tiniest mouthful of air.

"There it is." Grant found what he'd been looking for. He unfolded a large blanket on the open space of the floor. Grant met Nathan's tired gaze. "My commodities here are sparing, I'm afraid," he said.

"What did you do to me?" Nathan asked. "Why?"

Grant froze. "I saved your life."

"I'll be killed again. They'll find out; they'll kill me again. I can't..." Nathan's throat tightened. "I saw myself dead...and then." Nathan squeezed his eyes shut as he recalled the strange experience. *Was that a vision, or was that real?* "What am I now? What are you? I need answers, real ones."

Grant walked over to Nathan, pulled him to his feet, and guided him over to the blanket. The blanket was more comfortable than it looked. Grant pulled the edge of the blanket over Nathan's shoulders and sat on the floor in front of him. Nathan grabbed the end of the blanket with one hand to keep it from slipping. His shivers grew less intense.

"I injected the sap of a Neglia plant into your heart. I'll admit I wasn't entirely sure that it would work. It's known to extend human life expectancy. However, revival has only ever been recorded in ancient myths," Grant said.

"W-will I have side effects?"

"No. Not I'm aware of anyway."

Some of Nathan's worries eased, but the vision he'd seen still troubled him. "I'm broken, aren't I?"

"Where'd you get that idea?" Grant asked.

Nathan closed his eyes. "I saw something when I was dead. A reflection of myself, only it was wounded and...maybe not fully human. Somehow, that version of myself...it seemed too real like it wasn't just a reflection."

Grant took several moments of thoughtful silence before speaking. "You're not broken. Wounded, but capable of recovering. Think of it like a fractured bone, but on a deeper level. A hindrance for a time, but not permanent. I don't know what caused it, but I've suspected it for a long time."

"Suspected what exactly?"

Grant met Nathan's gaze. "A soul injury."

"You've suspected it but never said anything? That sounds serious."

"Inconvenient. Not serious. Otherwise, you wouldn't be here. It'll heal with time. Don't be surprised if your visions start coming more frequently or if you start developing other abilities." Grant said.

Nathan gritted his teeth as he recalled Lily's skepticism of Grant's motives. "What are you, Grant? Lily's right. I need to know. Why me, out of everyone else?"

Grant's gaze pierced Nathan without waiver. "You know why."

Nathan's gaze dropped. He did know. Several years back, a crowd of people attacked Grant, but Nathan had frightened the people away with magic. Nathan had snuck Grant into the Predual base to recover. While there, Grant noticed Nathan's interest in science and technology and offered to teach him.

"What do you think I am?" Grant asked.

"I'm...not sure."

"You've never been afraid of me, unlike most humans."

He's right, even the first time I met him. "There are depictions similar to your appearance in ancient hieroglyphics. Some texts describe the figures as gods of the time."

"Tsk, I am no god. I'm from the planet Notre. It's true our people have interacted in the past, though it's been a long time," Grant said.

Nathan gaped at Grant's words. While he'd expected an odd answer, he found himself unprepared for the one he got.

"My intent has always been to help you learn and grow as much as I can. You have the potential to become a great asset to your world."

"That's it? An asset to my world? This isn't my world. This world hates me." Anger and despair roiled from within Nathan and filled the air with static. The pale light of the electronics in the room flickered. He slouched as a tired dizziness buzzed in his head.

Grant placed a clawed hand on Nathan's shoulder. When he looked up, Grant studied his gaze with intense scrutiny.

Nathan managed a half-hearted grin, still fueled by anger. "Maybe the world would have been better off if you'd let me stay dead."

Grant looked away, but not before Nathan caught a glimpse of fear in his eyes. "Go to sleep. You've been through a lot recently, but you can't really believe that."

Nathan lay down and turned to face away from Grant. Despite his exhaustion, his mind continued to churn, weigh, and try to make sense of everything that happened. Only some part of Nathan did believe what he'd said.

Chapter 14

D aylight streamed down from a rectangular strip of a skylight near the entrance. Only the occasional chill ran through Nathan. His sleep had been fitful and disturbed by strange dreams.

Nathan climbed to his feet, relieved that their strength had returned. He walked, stood under the skylight, and looked up at the strip of blue sky visible through the glass. A glance at the door set the hair on his arms to rise. Nathan decided to put as much distance between himself and the exit as possible and crossed to the back of the room, where several electronics hummed gently. He lifted the smallest electronic device and turned it between his fingers to get a better look at the thing. Light, oval, made of an unfamiliar white metal, with three indentations that emitted a pale blue glow when touched.

A creak sounded nearby, and Grant emerged from a door previously hidden in shadow. "Be careful with that. Accidental activation of it might cause issues."

"What is it?" Nathan asked.

"It's an emergency communication device. It's only supposed to be used should something happen to me when my regular communicator has been damaged."

Nathan put the device back on the table.

"You said you're from another planet, right? Why come here of all places?"

"That's—" Grant's hand gripped the counter's edge, claws scraping the surface. "I'm here to investigate something."

"Which is?"

"A major energy fluctuation that originated from here." Grant released the counter, and his posture relaxed. "What happened yesterday? I thought you would be in recovery for a few more days."

Nathan released a held breath. *He's not going to tell me more.* "I wasn't. I need to finish my project, the teleporter. With the Union or this UGL trying to kill me, it's the only way I might escape. I have most of what I need, but I'm still missing some materials."

Grant met Nathan's gaze, an understanding in his eyes. "Let me see your blueprints. I want to be sure that everything's right and that you won't hurt yourself when you use the device."

Nathan nodded, sat on the floor, and took out his Spatial-box. He opened it to pull out the blueprints and materials. Grant sat next to Nathan.

"Do you still wish I hadn't revived you?" Grant asked.

Nathan winced. "I'm...not sure. It's too soon to ask me that."

"You told me not long ago that you didn't want to die. What changed?"

"Maybe the fact that I actually fucking died yesterday? Or that I'm likely to be killed again by the same people? What if I was meant to die? I just... What's the point if it goes nowhere?" Nathan's throat tightened. His nails dug into his own arms as tears blurred his vision.

"Nathan." Grant placed a hand on Nathan's back. "You didn't deserve to die yesterday. And no one's future is static. I will help you. You only ever seem to halfway believe me when I tell you, but I do mean it."

A small glimmer of hope reignited in Nathan's chest, and he struggled to pull himself back together. "I think...I'm going to need all the help I can get."

Grant picked up Nathan's blueprints' papers and data drives of from the floor. He flipped through some of the papers, before examining one of the data drives. "This isn't compatible with anything of mine. Don't you have a telecom I can read this with?"

Nathan dug through the Spatial-box again until he found his worn, cracked telecom. He handed the device to Grant.

Grant turned the telecom on and inserted the data drive. The screen flickered and wavered as if about to go out any second.

"I thought you had something better than this," Grant said.

"I did." Nathan's memory flitted to the night Summer stabbed him and left him for dead. "It got stolen."

Nathan reached for the black bracelet on his arm to look at it again.

"Grant, you seemed to know something about this." Nathan said, pointing at the bracelet. "What is it? And do you know if there's a way to remove it?"

Grant looked back up. "You can't take it off?"

Nathan shook his head.

"It was forged by Pontec with four condensed crystalloids of magic extracted from humans to give himself access to human magic. I don't know for sure how he did it, but considering the records of his behavior, it's likely the victims were subjected to some form of torture. Ah, I'm getting ahead of myself. You can't take it off. That doesn't seem right."

"I only had three stones," Nathan said.

"Fire, stone, and...ice?" Grant asked.

Nathan nodded.

"You could already use electricity naturally. I see what happened. Rather than binding to each other, they must have bonded directly to you. I doubt there's any way to remove it. Even if there is, I would avoid it. The process would likely be invasive and painful, if not deadly."

"Then I suppose I'm stuck with this now," Nathan said. *So much has changed.* "Grant? What was Pontec? I don't mean the shade I fought. I mean, when he still lived?"

Grant went silent for a long moment before he spoke. "Pontec was a member of a species called Maul. He was a Path-forger, which are very powerful beings. Because of that, he quickly rose to power and became a warlord. Many people and societies suffered from his quest to conquer those weaker than him. The real reason humans have had so few magic wielders for so long is because when Pontec lived, he killed almost all humans who possessed magic. His goal was to weaken every other dominant species but his own."

Nathan winced as he recalled his vision during the fight with Pontec's shade. "That's...not something else we should worry about, is it? Since Pontec is dead? And it happened a long time ago, right?"

"Pontec might be dead, but the Maul themselves aren't." Grant sighed. "I hope they won't become an issue anytime soon. For now, let's focus on our current problems."

Grant went back to looking over the materials and plans Nathan already had. After he finished, Grant stood up and walked to the door that led outside. "Stay here. I'll be back."

Nathan shivered as a gust of cold air blew through the room as Grant left.

After a bit of searching, Nathan found a bathroom where he took a warm shower. The shower took the edge off the lingering chill in his bones. Feeling a little closer to normal, he redressed, noticing his first pangs of hunger since yesterday. He searched around until he found a small fridge in a corner. He opened the fridge only to take a step back. The butchered remains of a dog lay in plain view. *That's weird.* He decided he wasn't hungry enough to risk anything in Grant's fridge.

He wondered where he might end up after he left the city. *I need to know more about the Union and this UGL, especially if they come looking for me.* Nathan remembered what Josh Black had said yesterday, that there was a database on West Street that would be empty on Tuesday night. Josh had said he'd help Nathan find it. That was tonight.

A chill crawled up Nathan's spine. He needed to know. He glanced at the door to outside and hoped that Grant would be back soon so he could tell him his plans.

Grant still hadn't come back. The small skylight in the ceiling was now dark with night. Nathan got up and walked to the door; he took a deep breath and turned the handle. Icy wind met him in an instant. His shoulders tensed against the cold as he stepped outside and closed the door again. Moonbeams touched the tops of the buildings to his right and the trees to his left.

Nathan turned into the city. His stomach knotted itself. He'd been given a taste of death only yesterday. Yet, here he was, going headfirst into another possible brush with it.

As he walked along the streets, a few people bustled past him in a hurry to wherever they were going, but none gave him a second glance. Relief washed through Nathan that either none of these people recognized him or else they didn't care.

By the time Nathan reached West Street, his body had adjusted to the cold temperature. He walked down West Street; there were no obvious entrances to the buildings on either side, though there was a section of wall where the brick looked more sunken than the rest. Nathan went to investigate it. Closer inspection revealed the sunken bricks to be an illusion. The bricks were larger but further back against the wall of a hallway that cut to the left and downward.

Nathan followed a cement stairwell down until he met a door with a hefty lock that appeared to take a key code. He lifted a hand to the lock; heat turned the metal to a red glow, and the melted gears dripped down the door and onto the cement floor. To Nathan's surprise, no alarms were set off. *What if Josh lied, and this is a trap?* Hands shaking, he pushed the door open and stepped into a linoleum-lined hallway with multiple doors.

Nathan melted the lock to the first room on his right. Inside the room, cabinets and counters lined two walls while four large machines sat in the center. Humid air chilled his skin. He took a couple of steps into the room and glanced back at the exit. *I'm already here. I need to at least try to find what I'm looking for.* He caught sight of a computer on the counter at the back of the room. He made his way toward it only to stop halfway next to one of the machines. Behind a shield of glass, a person lay inside, submerged in liquid. His physical build looked similar to Ivan's. Nathan backed up a couple of paces before he stopped and willed himself not to flee.

He forced himself past the machines and reached the computer at the back of the room. After looking through the computer, disappointment sank into his chest. The computer only seemed to hold monitoring information on the people being held in the machines. There wasn't anything relevant to what he was looking for.

Nathan drew away from the computer and quickly left the room. Back in the hallway, he wondered how he would find the info he wanted. He swallowed a hard lump of fear in his throat and pressed farther down the hallway, deeper into the Union.

The sickly dim glow of fluorescent lights and the steady buzz of poor electrical wiring set his teeth on edge.

He took a turn into a branching hallway. He hoped he'd find some sort of staff room. *What if I don't? Is what I've already seen here really enough?* He doubted those people in the machines were here voluntarily. They were clearly test subjects of the Union for something. Nathan could already piece together that maybe he, or his parents, may have been here once.

He'd almost lost track of how far in he'd gone when he came across a partially opened door. The floor was carpeted, unlike anywhere else in the building. He pushed the door open a little wider. The lighting glowed softer inside; a sizeable oval desk stood in the center of the room, and the walls were lined with shelves and file holders.

Nathan made his way over to the desk and began searching for anything that might have UGL data on it. None of the drawers had anything of relevance to him at first glance. He decided to dou-ble-check, just in case, and this time, he noticed a thin lockbox of the same color as the inside of the desk in the bottom right drawer. He pulled the lockbox out and placed a hand over the lock; his hand grew warm as he melted the lock away. He pried the box open and took out a thin, flat tablet-like device.

The loud bang of a door slamming shut somewhere in the build-ing sent a jolt of fear up Nathan's spine. His hands shook as he took his spatial-box from his pocket and stuffed the UGL's tablet inside it.

Nathan stood up. He didn't know if the tablet held the information he wanted, but he needed to get out now before anyone found him there. He made his way back to the door, which opened before he reached it.

Nathan's breath caught in his chest. He recognized the man who stood in the doorway.

Nathan backed away from Ivan's looming figure. His blood pounded through his veins. Ivan stepped through the doorway and closed the door.

"You again," Ivan said.

This was a mistake. Nathan clasped his sai as he continued to back away. He wished he owned a more effective weapon.

Ivan carried the same spiked club as yesterday. Nathan despised the thing.

"Your body was gone when they went to get it. Josh Black spilled the rest."

Ivan swung the club through the air at Nathan. Nathan raised his hand. Sparks formed as electricity crackled from his hand. The cyan snakes of magic connected with the club's metal spikes.

Fuck this thing. Nathan used the polarization to fling the club from Ivan's hand. It flew behind Ivan to slam against the door window. The rectangular window shattered as the club clattered to the floor.

Ivan pulled out a long, serrated blade.

Nathan grabbed his sai to block it as Ivan swiped the blade at him. Nathan gritted his teeth at the harsh zip of the serrated metal as it slid against the sai. He threw a hand up. A wall of ice formed between Ivan and himself. A breath of relief escaped him too soon. Ivan shattered the wall with a single punch and launched himself at Nathan. Pain shot up Nathan's spine as he found himself pressed beneath the huge man's weight.

"You got me in trouble. I'll make sure you're dead this time."

Nathan managed to lift his sai in time to block a stab aimed at Ivan's neck. *Not this time.* Nathan dropped a sai and grabbed the arm Ivan held him with. Fire sparked to life under his fingers. Ivan's flesh grew hot, and blood ran down his hand.

Nathan wriggled out of Ivan's grip and successfully blocked the next swipes of the blade. Ivan swung a fist at him and missed. Ivan's eyes widened as he gazed at his burnt, bleeding hand. He lunged at Nathan with a set grimace.

"Ack."

Nathan stumbled back and pressed a hand to his stomach. Blood flowed out, unconstrained by Nathan's attempt to staunch it.

He looked up to see Ivan's grimace change into an unsettling grin. Ivan took another slash at Nathan. A new wound opened in Nathan's arm, deep enough for him to have a glimpse of bone before blood covered it. Ivan shoved Nathan back to the ground.

I can't die again. Nathan fought to shake his daze off through the shock. Panic lighted in his mind as Ivan ripped Nathan's hand away from his wound. Ivan dug his fingers into Nathan's flesh and tore the wound wider. Nathan screamed. His nerves heated as his magic came to life and he spun a stone stake out of the air. Clutching the stake he thrust it into Ivan's torso. This time, Ivan reacted to the injury, freezing in place.

Nathan feebly dragged himself away from Ivan. When Nathan glanced back, Ivan stared down at the stake in his chest. The rod sat wedged in his diaphragm, which meant he likely couldn't breathe. Ivan's eyes looked up back at Nathan hardening. The huge man rose from the ground.

Refusing to give up, Nathan gathered his strength and released one last powerful shock wave of electricity. Ivan staggered back to the ground and did not get up.

Nathan groaned and pressed his injured arm against his stomach using his good arm to pull himself closer to the exit. His vision faded and returned. He panted from the effort to stay awake. He'd already lost too much blood.

The door to the room opened. Nathan closed his eyes and clenched his teeth. Of course, Ivan wouldn't have been the only Union agent to come. It was over for him.

"Shit. Nathan?"

Nathan dared to look back up. He knew that deep voice.

Grant flipped Nathan over and pressed his hand firmly against the slice in Nathan's stomach to stanch the blood flow.

"Why'd you come here? Why didn't you tell me you were coming here?"

"I had to...." His vision bleared and grew spottier as he broke into a cold sweat. "If I...don't... Not again..." Were the best he could manage to get out.

"You're not going to die again," Grant said.

He lifted Nathan off the ground. A fleeting sense of comfort spread through him before the distorting motion of being picked up darkened his sight.

Chapter 15

Nathan woke in a now familiar room. A sense of relief rushed through him. He'd survived. Achy weakness tugged at his body, but he inched up slowly and examined the array of stitches across his abdomen and arm. Somehow, sitting up didn't hurt as bad as he'd expected. *I must have been given pain meds.* Several lines of IV ran into the same arm with stitches. A dizzying pressure formed in his head, and Nathan's vision started to tunnel. He lay back down and took several controlled breaths until his sight cleared.

Movement in the corner of the room caught Nathan's attention.

"Seems you're awake. What kind of stunt were you trying to pull?" Grant asked.

"I...wanted to know why those people wanted me dead. I meant to tell you but didn't know when you'd be back. I didn't want to miss the opportunity to find out," Nathan said. "It was reckless. I'm sorry."

"Did you find what you were looking for?"

"Yes. At least, I think so. Where's my stuff?" Nathan asked.

Grant stood and opened a drawer across the room. "What do you need?"

"My Spatial-box, the gold chest."

Grant brought it over to Nathan.

Nathan opened it and found the thin tablet inside. He turned the device on and then realized it had a lock code. Nathan closed his eyes to better focus and activated his magic. A light electrical current ran down his arm to his fingers and the device he held. He succeeded in bypassing the lock code and proceeded to search for UGL files on the tablet. He found a file that seemed to be what he was after and searched for his own name in the database.

"Hey, Grant. Can I have a few moments to myself?" Nathan asked.

Grant nodded and left the room.

As Nathan read through the more in-depth info on the tablet, cold shivers ran through him. His stomach twisted into near-painful knots at what he had learned. He'd been used as a test subject by the UGL or Union of Greater Laboratories. Both him and his mother. Something had gone wrong in the early stages of the experiment, and Nathan's status was changed from ground soldier to field agent. He'd been allowed to be raised outside the laboratory to gain social skills, though he'd been meant to be brought back at age twelve. He'd gone MIA when they went to collect him. Now, they wanted him dead because he wasn't conditioned into the mentality they wanted.

Nathan looked up and put the tablet down as Dr. Bailey entered the room. "You look a lot better than you did," Bailey said.

"You knew. You could have told me," Nathan said. "You could have told me what I was this whole time but didn't."

Dr. Bailey froze. "Told you what?"

"That I'm a UGL experiment gone wrong that you were involved with."

Bailey's gaze found the tablet in Nathan's lap. "How did you get that?"

"How do you think? Why didn't you tell me? I wouldn't have been poisoned, killed, and nearly killed again if you'd just told me."

"No, I couldn't, even though I wanted to."

"Why not?"

Bailey went silent for a long moment his brow creasing.

"Nathan...I got out of the UGL. I was allowed to retire. That's a rare privilege. I was so tired of it, of everything that happens in there. The conditions for my retirement are under a gag order. If the UGL finds out I've slipped info, I could be forced back to the lab either as a working prisoner, a test subject myself, or killed if I got lucky."

"And yes, I was involved with the experiment on you. I only had a year left before retirement when your mother arrived. She was terrified for you and begged me not to let them ruin you. I couldn't fully go against orders, but I did what I could. I tampered with the equipment and substituted for placebos instead. It caused the experiment to fail, mostly. I can't say how much you may have been affected after I left, but you're clearly more resilient than the average person."

Nathan's breath shook, and he looked away from Bailey.

"I never expected to see you again. It was a shock when you showed up here."

"Guess I should thank you for not turning me in," Nathan said, still unable to look at him.

"I would never hand someone over to them." Bailey's already gruff voice hardened.

Nathan's throat tightened. He knew Bailey was telling him the truth.

"You should rest. I know you must feel like shit. You really needed a blood transfusion, but I couldn't find a match, not even your mother," Bailey said.

"My mother? You know where she is?" Nathan asked.

"She's not exactly... She's in an asylum."

"I know that much. Which one?"

"You can't go there. Not if you want to stay alive anyway. Not unless something drastic changes."

"I...I need a minute," Nathan said.

Bailey's grimace eased a little, and he left.

Nathan took a deep inhale and released it slowly. Bailey didn't tell him out of fear. Mark joined and left out of fear. Summer tried to kill him out of fear. *Everyone is so sick and fearful. This isn't a world I want to live in.* Nathan's fists clenched the constriction in his throat threatening to bring tears.

"I couldn't help but overhear."

Nathan looked up to see Grant's tall, dark figure in the doorway.

"Did you know any of that before now?" Nathan asked.

Grant walked over placing his clawed hand on the bed rail.

"I knew of the UGL. I didn't know you'd been a test subject of theirs."

"How? You've not worked for them, too, have you?"

Grant shook his head. "No. Never. I've been investigating certain matters. The UGL being one of them."

Nathan wanted to ask more but let himself fall silent. He didn't want to pressure Grant after he'd been so much more open than he used to be. Nathan's mind wandered back to his plan to escape the city. "I should finish my project."

"Yes. I got the materials you didn't have." Grant paused for a moment. "I have to leave in a couple days. I worry about you."

"You're leaving?" A cold stone formed in Nathan's stomach. "Where? For how long?"

"My home. It should only be a few weeks. Though a lot can happen in that time," Grant said.

"I'll try to lay low," Nathan said. He meant it this time.

Nathan glanced back down at the telecom's screen. A lump formed in his throat. His father's constant blame that Nathan ruined his life and his mother's mental breaking—those made sense now.

Grant held a packet out to Nathan, interrupting his thoughts. Nathan took it and opened it to discover more materials than he needed.

"A little overboard, but thank you," Nathan said.

"I brought excess on purpose," Grant said. "Making a spare wouldn't hurt."

"I'll consider it," Nathan said.

Evening shadows stretched in the corners of the dining room where Lily sat reading at the table. The door to the house clicked open. Lily stood up in alarm as a woman barged in. Tall, with long blond curls, and a silver, gold trimmed sword on her hip. Recognition dawned on Lily. Summer, the person who stabbed Nathan the night Mark called her for help, and later ordered the Predual fight that injured Mark.

"Hi, um, are you having an emergency? We're a private clinic. Outside of emergencies we prefer if you called ahead."

Lily gave her best customer service grin but lifted a scrunched rod from the chair next to her and stepped out in front of Summer.

"Hello to you, too."

Summer held her hands out to show they were empty. Not convincing considering the sword, and a long knife which hung at her leg which Lily had overlooked at first. Lily imagined Summer could snatch it up in a second if she wanted.

"What brings you here?" As if Lily couldn't guess.

"I heard a rumor that Nathan's here. Is he?"

Lily stiffened. "Nathan? Are you a relative? Do you have a last name?"

She reached for a tablet on the table.

"I can look them up to see if they're here and ask if they're expecting you."

"Don't play dumb. This place is way too small for you to not know your patients, plus I know you know him, and at least know of me," Summer said.

"He's not here." Lily glanced away.

"Really?" Summer's foot tapped the floor a few times, and she fidgeted before letting her shoulders drop. "You know that one night? My friends told me one of your friends got hurt. I didn't want to drag you or your friends into it, but I could see you'd get in the way. I only wanted Nathan..."

"Why do you want to kill him? Did he wrong you or something?"

Summer looked at the floor and choked out a single laugh. "No. But we live in a real fucked-up world, you know. And I'm just trying to keep other people safe for the fucked-up price of a life."

She turned to the door. "Anyway, I'm leaving. If Nathan is here, though... He shouldn't be, for your own sake."

Lily watched as the door closed behind Summer. Tremors ran through her body as she allowed her tension to leave, and new worries fell into place.

Lily locked the front door and went into the hallway to Nathan's room. She entered the room, where papers, wires, and gadget bits lay on the bedside table. Nathan lay asleep.

She knew better than to wake patients, especially ones injured as badly as he was, but this was important. She walked over and nudged Nathan's shoulder. Nathan woke up with a start, and his breath quickened. His teeth showed, clenched together as he started to sit forward.

"No, you don't need to move," Lily said.

Nathan relaxed a little. "What is it?" he asked.

Lily couldn't help but notice how frail Nathan still seemed. *I shouldn't have woken him.* "Summer was here just minutes ago. She was looking for you. I told her you weren't here, but she didn't seem convinced."

Nathan's gaze averted away from her. "I probably don't have much time then. I wouldn't put it past her to give away my location. I'll have to leave soon."

There were blood spots on the sheet that covered Nathan. "You should try to stay as long as possible. If you don't rest, your wounds will take longer to heal," Lily said. "Speaking of which, can I?"

"Sure." Nathan nodded.

Lily placed a hand over his torso. A pink light glowed in her hand. A few minutes later, Lily grabbed a pair of scissors to remove a couple of no longer needed stitches.

"Your magic's improved, hasn't it?" Nathan asked.

Lily knew he was right. "I think so," she said. She sat next to Nathan's bed and ran both hands through her long auburn hair. "The day that you died...I found you on my way back. I didn't think anything could be done. That creature... Grant. He made me heal you. I was shocked it even worked. It was...actually easier than healing a living person, you know, but it still took a long time. Grant, he injected you with something. Did he tell you what it was? Did he do anything else to you?"

"He did tell me about it," Nathan said. "Look, I realize Grant is different, very different. But I've known him several years, and he's never given me a reason to think he would harm me."

Lily nodded, though she wasn't sure she agreed with Nathan's judgment.

Over the next several days, as Nathan healed, he began the construction of the teleporter. He sat in Bailey's patients' room while he put the finishing touches on the teleporters. *Where will I even go? Maybe Opal like Bailey suggested? Is it any safer than here?* The more cryptic part of his mind questioned if anything had been worth it. Whether he would have been better off dying back when Summer shoved that dagger into his ribs or if Grant hadn't had the means to revive him. He shook his head trying to shove those thoughts away, but they continued to fester.

Nathan placed two small teleporters down in front of him. They were almost finished. He'd taken Grant's advice of making a backup, just in case. Nathan placed a hand over them and closed his eyes as a trickle of energy ran down his arm to infuse the teleporters with a spark of magic. Now they should be ready.

Nathan swallowed, his pulse quickening as a rush of anxiety engulfed him. The time was here, to leave the city, to start somewhere fresh, and maybe have a better quality of life, just like he'd wanted for so many years. He hoped he'd be able to focus more on his inventions in the future. Living in a cleaner environment than where he'd been for so long during his time with the Preduals would be ideal. Yet, Nathan hesitated. The idea seemed too surreal.

Nathan took a deep breath and fastened one of the teleporters onto his wrist.

Lily stepped into the room. "Oh, it looks like you finished that," she said. "Have you decided where you're going?"

Nathan gave a light shrug. "Not really."

"Mark called me earlier. He asked about you."

"What did you tell him? Is he okay?" Nathan asked.

"I didn't know how to tell him everything. I told him you'd been hurt but are recovering and will probably leave in a day or two," Lily said. "As far as I could tell, Mark sounded fine." Her gaze wandered back to the teleporter. "Is it actually safe to use that?"

"I really hope so," Nathan said.

Both Nathan and Lily started when a loud bang echoed through the house as a door slammed open.

"What do you think you're doing here?" That was Dr. Bailey's voice.

"I have a warrant to search the place."

Carson. Nathan recognized the voice. His blood turned to ice.

"On what grounds?" Bailey asked.

"I think you already know," Carson said.

Nathan wondered if he should help and took a step forward. Lily grabbed his arm to stop him.

"We'll be okay. You need to go," she said. Lily moved past him and stepped out of the room into the hallway. "Dr. Bailey, what's going on?" she asked.

She's trying to buy time. Nathan gathered together his few things and then reached to activate the teleporter. The teleporter emanated a blue glow as it came to life.

"I knew it." Carson appeared in the doorway. He raised a gun. Nathan flinched. A flash and loud bang followed.

A hollow ache drew Nathan's gaze to his wrist. A faint dizziness tore at him. Bits of the teleporter hung loose, broken. A faint glow still emanated from it, though. The immediate world around Nathan wisped away into something colder.